REA

RUN FOR YOUR WIFE

by

Ray Cooney

D0803976

SAMUEL FRENCH, INC.
45 WEST 25th STREET   NEW YORK 10010
7623 SUNSET BOULEVARD   HOLLYWOOD 90046
LONDON   *TORONTO*

Copyright © 1984, 1990 by Salina and I

ISBN 0 573 69189 4   Printed in U.S.A.

IMPORTANT BILLING AND CREDIT REQUIREMENTS

Run For Your Wife was first produced at the Yvonne Arnaud Theatre, Guildford, on 26th October, 1982, with the following cast:

MARY SMITH..Carol Hawkins
BARBARA SMITH ....Helen Gill
JOHN SMITH..Ray Cooney
DETECTIVE SERGEANT TROUGHTON
....Peter Blake
STANLEY GARDNER ....Royce Mills
NEWSPAPER REPORTER..........................Arthur Bostrum
DETECTIVE SERGEANT PORTERHOUSE
....Bill Pertwee
BOBBY FRANKLYN............................Jimmy Thompson

Directed by Ray Cooney
Designed by Douglas Heap
Lighting by James Baird

The play was subsequently produced by The Theatre of Comedy Company at the Shaftesbury Theatre, London, on 29th March, 1983, with the following cast:

MARY SMITH..Carol Hawkins
BARBARA SMITH ....Helen Gill
JOHN SMITH.. Richard Briers
DETECTIVE SERGEANT TROUGHTON
....Peter Blake
STANLEY GARDNER ....Bernard Cribbins
NEWSPAPER REPORTER....................................Sam Cox
DETECTIVE SERGEANT PORTERHOUSE
....Bill Pertwee
BOBBY FRANKLYN....................................Royce Mills

Directed by Ray Cooney
Designed by Douglas Heap
Lighting by James Baird

Run For Your Wife was first produced by The Theatre of Comedy presented by Don Taffner, Paul Elliott and Strada Entertainment Trust at the Virginia Theatre, New York City, on March 7, 1989 with the following cast:

JOHN SMITH ....Ray Cooney
DETECTIVE SERGEANT TROUGHTON
.... Gareth Hunt
BARBARA HUNT.................................. Hilary Labow
DETECTIVE SERGEANT PORTERHOUSE
.... Dennis Ramsden
BOBBY FRANKLYN................................ Gavin Reed
THE REPORTER...................................Doug Stender
MARY SMITH .... Kay Walbye
STANLEY GARDNER......................Paxton Whitehead

Directed by Ray Cooney
Set Supervision by Michael Anania
Costumes by Joseph G. Aulisi
Lighting by Marilyn Rennagel
Production Stage Manager was Amy Pell

CHARACTERS

(in order of appearance)

MARY SMITH	A short and attractive blonde in her late twenties.
BARBARA SMITH	A tall and attractive red-head in her mid-twenties.
JOHN SMITH	An ordinary looking man whose appearance belies his eccentricity.
DETECTIVE SERGEANT TROUGHTON	A slightly severe young officer.
STANLEY GARDNER	A bright fellow whose "brightness" is only skin deep.
NEWSPAPER REPORTER	A large gentleman.
DETECTIVE SERGEANT PORTERHOUSE	A middle-aged family man.
BOBBY FRANKLYN	A flamboyant dress designer of indeterminate age.

AUTHOR'S NOTE

The action of the play takes place in the home of John and Mary Smith in Wimbledon and the home of John and Barbara Smith in Streatham. In the main, the set, which is the lounge of a modern flat, "doubles" for both homes. Frequently, throughout the play action will be taking place simultaneously in each of the flats but the inhabitants of each flat are, naturally, oblivious to the others.

There is a door ULC in the rear wall which leads into Mary's hall and a door URC in the rear wall which leads to Barbara's hall. The decor of the area ULC represents Mary's home and the decor of the area URC which is totally different, represents Barbara's home. There is a window in the left wall UL which has Mary's curtains and a window in the right wall UR which has Barbara's curtains (or venetian blinds). The remainder of the lounge (about two-thirds of the total area) "doubles" for both homes. There is a door DL leading to the kitchen(s)—offstage can be seen a modern kitchen; and a door DR leading to the bedroom(s)—offstage can be seen a double bed and a dressing-table.

Down centre is a long settee (with arms) and at either end is a table on each of which there is a telephone. Behind the settee is a table which is almost as high as the settee. There are two armchairs, one DLC and one DRC. Also in the "communal" area are two wastebins, which are beside each of the armchairs. In the "communal" area the only items not "doubled" are the two telephones, the one on the table left of the settee being "Mary's" and the one on the table right of the settee being Barbara's.

In the "communal" area there can be paintings, plants and other dressings on the walls but nowhere in any area of the set are there any "family" photographs.

In the London production Mary's area UL including the carpet, was "blue", Barbara's area UR was "yellow" and the "communal" area was "green" (with the exception of Mary's telephone which was blue and Barbara's which was yellow. The settee, armchairs and cushions in the "communal" area were of ranging shades of green. Again, in the London production, Mary's and Barbara's upstage areas were on a slightly raised level (approximately 9 inch rostrum) and there was a step down into the "communal" area.

The two front doorbells should sound different as should the telephone bells.

The play is in two acts. The action is continuous and takes place one sunny summer morning.

N.B.

(1) All stage directions are given from the actors' point of view.

(2) Each telephone has a long extension to its socket to enable the actors to move around whilst holding the telephone.

ACT I

Curtain up Music — Orchestral version of "Love and Marriage[*]*"*

The curtain rises on an empty stage. The curtains of both windows are drawn but there are shafts of the early morning sun sneaking through into the semi-darkness. The music continues through the entire following sequence. After a moment MARY enters from kitchen D.L. SHE is in her nightgown and carrying a mug of tea. SHE looks at her watch, then puts her mug on table behind settee, and goes up to window U.L. SHE opens the curtains and the SUN streams in lighting up the U.L. area and some of the "communal" area. MARY looks out of her window (her husband is late home.) SHE then hesitates a moment and hurries down to their telephone on table L of settee. SHE starts to dial "100" but then hesitates and replaces receiver. As MARY looks at her watch again BARBARA enters from the bedroom D.R. BARBARA is wearing a long flowing negligee and carrying a breakfast tray. MARY hurries up to her window again and looks out as BARBARA closes the bedroom door and moves up to behind settee. As BARBARA puts her tray down on table behind settee MARY has returned from her window and picked up her mug of tea. BARBARA and MARY, standing side by side, each look at their watches simultaneously—it is clear that they are not aware of each other (which is as it should be because Mary is in Wimbledon and Barbara is in Streatham).

---

[*] See cautionary note in front matter.

9

BARBARA hurries up to her window U.R. as MARY moves to her phone on table L of settee. MARY starts to dial "100" yet again but changes her mind once more and moves in front of settee towards bedroom D.R. Whilst Mary has been doing this BARBARA has opened her curtains (or blinds) and SUNLIGHT has flooded the U.R. area and the remainder of the "communal" area the whole stage is now bathed in bright warm LIGHT. BARBARA has opened her window, looked out, closed her window and moved down to her telephone on table R. of settee. Both MARY and BARBARA hesitate and once more, in unison (but oblivious of each other!) look at their watches. MARY exits into bedroom still carrying her mug of tea as BARBARA starts to dial "100" (her husband is late home). BARBARA decides against calling the police, replaces the phone, picks up her tray from table above settee and exits into kitchen as MARY returns from bedroom. She is now wearing a dressing gown. MARY closes bedroom door and moves up to her window UL as BARBARA returns from kitchen carrying a "squeegy" washing up liquid. BARBARA puts "squeegy" on table behind settee, goes to the window and looks out. MARY and BARBARA both move away from their windows wondering what to do. In unison THEY each go to their hall door (MARY ULC and BARBARA URC) and look out. THEY both close their door and stand there for a moment wondering what to do. THEY decide—in unison—to hurry to their telephones (MARY L of settee, BARBARA R of settee) and dial "100". Having dialled THEY sit at either end of the settee, MARY L. and BARBARA R, waiting for the operator to answer. AS THEY sit the MUSIC fades. [N.B. The entire sequence above is taken at quite a pace as both girls are in a state of nervous tension.])

MARY. (*On phone.*) Operator, do you think you could get me Wimbledon Police Station, please–

BARBARA. (*On phone.*) Operator–?

MARY. (*On phone.*) Thank you.

BARBARA. (*On phone.*) Could you put me through to Streatham Police Station, please–

MARY. (*On phone.*) Hello?

BARBARA. (*On phone.*) Thank you.

MARY. (*On phone.*) Is that Wimbledon Police Station? ... I'm sorry to trouble you, Sergeant, but I'm a bit worried about my husband.

BARBARA. (*On phone.*) Streatham Police? I'm rather concerned about my husband?

MARY/BARBARA. (*Together, on phone.*) Mr. John Smith.

MARY. (*On phone.*) I'm Mrs. Mary Smith.

BARBARA. (*On phone.*) Barbara Smith.

MARY. (*On phone.*) Number 25.

BARBARA. (*On phone.*) Number 47.

MARY. (*On phone.*) Kenilworth Avenue.

BARBARA. (*On phone.*) Lewin Road.

MARY. (*On phone.*) Wimbledon.

BARBARA. (*On phone.*) Streatham.

MARY. (*On phone.*) London, S.W. 19.

BARBARA. (*On phone.*) London, S.W. 16.

MARY. (*On phone.*) John Smith, that's right. He's a taxi driver.

BARBARA. (*On phone.*) He's a taxi driver.

MARY. (*On phone.*) I woke up this morning and he hadn't come home. He was due back at 12 o'clock last night.

BARBARA. (*On phone.*) He was due back this morning at 7:30.

MARY. (*On phone.*) From the Night Shift.

BARBARA. (*On phone.*) From the early shift. It's gone 8:30 and he's always so punctual.

MARY. (*On phone.*) I wouldn't worry except that he keeps to a very exact schedule.

BARBARA. He has this very precise schedule, you see.

MARY. (*On phone.*) But he does put in a lot of overtime. I'm worried–

BARBARA/MARY. (*Together, on phone.*) He might have fallen asleep at the wheel of his taxi.

BARBARA. (*On phone.*) Hospitals?

MARY. (*On phone.*) No, I haven't.

BARBARA. (*On phone.*) Would you?

MARY. (*On phone.*) Thank you very much.

BARBARA. (*On phone.*) I'm very grateful.

MARY. (*On phone.*) Well, he's sort of commonplace really.

BARBARA. (*On phone.*) Average, I suppose.

MARY/BARBARA. (*Together, on phone.*) Medium height, brown hair, blue eyes—sort of cuddly.

MARY. (*On phone.*) Distinguishing marks?

BARBARA. (*On phone.*) Not really.

MARY. (*On phone.*) No.

BARBARA/MARY. (*Together on phone.*) He's very ordinary ... Thank you.

(*BARBARA and MARY each put down their phone and think for a moment. Mary's DOORBELL is heard off. MARY reacts and hurries out into her hall, ULC. During the ensuing dialogue BARBARA goes up to her window and looks out. SHE then picks up her "squeegy" from the table above settee and exits DL into kitchen.*)

MARY. (*Off.*) Oh, my goodness!

JOHN. (*Off.*) Hello!

TROUGHTON. (*Off.*) He'll be all right, Madam.
MARY. (*As THEY enter.*) I knew he'd had an accident.
TROUGHTON. Steady as we go.

(*TROUGHTON, in plain clothes, and MARY enter supporting a bedraggled John who is casually dressed in slacks and loose fitting zip-jacket. JOHN's head is swathed in a bandage and although he's a bit groggy, he is trying to be bright. During the following dialogue MARY leads JOHN to the settee and generally "fusses" over him, although in her relief she treats him like an errant schoolboy. MARY sits R of settee, JOHN sits C of settee and TROUGHTON stands DLC.*)

MARY. Poor darling!
JOHN. I'm fine.
TROUGHTON. On the settee.
JOHN. I'm O.K. Honest.
MARY. Look at the state of him. Sweetheart!

(*BARBARA has exited into kitchen by now.*)

TROUGHTON. (*To Mary.*) Detective Sergeant Troughton—Wimbledon Police.

MARY. I've just been on the phone to your Police Station.

TROUGHTON. I wouldn't know about that, Mrs. Smith. I've been with your husband at Wimbledon Hospital for the last three hours.

MARY. (*Tersely.*) Oh, John! I got the shock of my life when I woke up this morning and you weren't there. (*To Troughton.*) He's never not been there. What on earth happened, Sergeant?

(*MARY surveys John's bandaged head.*)

TROUGHTON. Well, it seems your husband got involved with a couple of young villains, (*To John.*) didn't you?

JOHN. (*Nodding brightly.*) Yes.

MARY. (*Tersely.*) Oh, John! You'd better have a cup of coffee, sweetheart.

JOHN. (*Nods.*) Coffee.

(*BARBARA returns from kitchen and closes door.*)

MARY. All right to give him a cup of coffee, Sergeant?

TROUGHTON. Yes, he's a bit groggy, that's all.

MARY. (*Tersely.*) Oh, John!

BARBARA. (*Looking at watch, tersely.*) Oh, John! (*BARBARA, having said the above remark, whilst passing Troughton [who, of course does not react] hurries into the bedroom, closing the door.*)

MARY. Coffee for you, Sergeant?

TROUGHTON. No thanks, Mrs. Smith. Oh, the hospital said your husband had to take these tablets.

(*TROUGHTON takes bottle of pills from his pocket and hands them across John to Mary. JOHN tries to "focus" on the pills and continues to smile rather blankly.*)

TROUGHTON. Just to ease the headache, I think. One tablet, twice a day.

MARY. (*To John.*) Poor darling.

JOHN. (*Nods.*) Yes.

MARY. Have you had any breakfast?

JOHN. (*Shakes his head.*) No.

MARY. Do you want a nice little egg?

JOHN. (*Shakes his head.*) No thank you.

(MARY crosses in front of Troughton to kitchen door.)

MARY. *(To Troughton.)* I'll get his coffee then. It was really very good of you to drive him back home.

TROUGHTON. *(Grins.)* He's in no fit state, is he? I must admit I quite enjoyed sitting behind the wheel of his taxi. Lovely feeling of power, driving along with the light on, ignoring people trying to wave me down.

MARY. I'm most grateful.

TROUGHTON. Least we could do. Your husband's a hero, aren't you, Mr. Smith?

JOHN. *(Brightly nodding.)* Yes!

MARY. It's so unlike him to do anything spectacular.

TROUGHTON. He "had a go," Mrs. Smith. Didn't you?

JOHN. *(Smiling blankly.)* Yes!

MARY. He's a silly fool. *(Exits into kitchen.)*

TROUGHTON. *(Takes out his notebook.)* I won't stay long, sir. I'd just like to clarify a couple of points.

JOHN. Right!

(During the ensuing speech JOHN looks 'round the room trying to take it all in, whilst TROUGHTON walks around the back of the settee and DRC.)

TROUGHTON. Now then. *(Refers to notebook.)* Last night—approximately 23:00 hours—*(Smiles at John.)* that's 11:00 p.m.—you were driving your taxi. It *is* your taxi, sir. You're the proprietor as it were? The owner-driver?

JOHN. Excuse me, what time is it?

(TROUGHTON stops by chair DR.)

TROUGHTON. (*Surprised.*) Quarter to nine, sir.

JOHN. (*Trying to work it out.*) Quarter to nine.

TROUGHTON. (*Moves to settee and sits on R. arm.*) So back to 11 p.m. last night, sir. When you got involved with this mugging incident.

JOHN. Mugging. Yes.

TROUGHTON. (*Refers to notes.*) You were driving home to Wimbledon with an empty cab.

JOHN. (*Worried but still hazy.*) Quarter to nine in the *morning?*

TROUGHTON. That's right. (*Refers to notes.*) And as you were passing Wimbledon Underground Station, you saw an old lady struggling with two youths.

JOHN. Wednesday morning?

TROUGHTON. Yes.

JOHN. What happened to Tuesday night?

TROUGHTON. Well, half of it you spent at Wimbledon Police Station and half at Wimbledon Hospital.

JOHN. (*Thinking.*) Schedule.

TROUGHTON. Beg pardon?

JOHN. (*Trying to pull himself together.*) I think I'm out on my schedule.

TROUGHTON. I'm not surprised.

JOHN. (*Looking around.*) This is Wimbledon.

TROUGHTON. (*Bemused.*) That's right.

JOHN. (*Looks towards kitchen.*) That was Mary.

TROUGHTON. Yes, she's just making some coffee.

(*JOHN quickly takes his diary from inside pocket of his jacket and flicks through the pages to check on his "schedule."*)

TROUGHTON. (*Referring to notes.*) Wimbledon Underground Station. Two youths attempting to relieve an old lady of her handbag.

JOHN. (*Reads from diary.*) Barbara. 7:30 a.m.

TROUGHTON. No. Doreen Spinks, 23:00 hours.

(*MARY comes in from kitchen with mug of coffee. JOHN puts diary away and immediately gives Mary a huge smile and opens his arms to her. Mary has left John's bottle of pills in the kitchen.*)

TROUGHTON. Mrs. Spinks is struggling with two youths. You stop your taxi and rush to her assistance.

MARY. Oh, John, you might have got yourself killed.

JOHN. Hang on a second. I'm trying to work something out.

(*MARY crosses to the L of settee, puts John's coffee on table and removes his jacket.*)

MARY. You're going to bed, that's what you're doing. (*To Troughton.*) He's really in no fit state to be answering questions. How come you didn't sort all this out last night?

(*During the ensuing speech MARY puts John's jacket on back of settee and gives him his coffee.*)

TROUGHTON. (*Rising.*) Because Mr. Smith wasn't very co-operative last night. To start with he wouldn't tell us who he was. And then he wouldn't tell us where he lived. And what with this hysterical old girl and Mr. Smith fainting every five minutes.

MARY. Oh, John!

TROUGHTON. It was quite a "to-do." (*To John.*) Just a couple of questions, sir, then I'll be off.

(*TROUGHTON sits on the R arm of settee.*)

JOHN. Right! My taxi's outside, isn't it?

TROUGHTON. Yes, sir.

JOHN. Good.

TROUGHTON. Now, you intervened in the struggle—

JOHN. Yes.

MARY. Silly fool!

TROUGHTON. Mrs. Smith.

MARY. Well, he went and got himself attacked by these two brutes.

JOHN. No, I didn't. The old lady hit me with her handbag.

MARY. What? Silly cow!

TROUGHTON. Mrs. Smith!

JOHN. She thought I was with the two blokes, you see.

TROUGHTON. We *know* that, Mr. Smith. Now, the two youths ran off?

JOHN. Yes. Down Wimbledon High Street.

TROUGHTON. O.K. Now can you give us a description?

JOHN. (*Thinking hard.*) It's a main road with shops on both sides–

TROUGHTON. Of the two youths!

JOHN. It was so quick. What with the old woman belting me about the head and me trying to explain I was just a passing taxi driver—

MARY. You should mind your own business!

(*There is the sound of Mary's front DOORBELL.*)

MARY. Excuse me, Sergeant. (*Exits her hall ULC.*)

JOHN. (*Looking at watch.*) Is that all now? I'd really like to be off.

TROUGHTON. There is one tiny point, sir.

JOHN. Oh yes?

TROUGHTON. Slight confusion. At Wimbledon Police Station you gave your address—when you finally agreed to volunteer that information and in between fainting—you gave your address as here—(*HE refers to notes.*) —25 Kenilworth Avenue, Wimbledon, S.W. 19.

JOHN. Yes.

TROUGHTON. (*Sits beside John on the settee.*) But–er–the hospital somehow seems to have got your address as–er–(*He refers to notes.*)–47 Lewin Road, Streatham, S.W. 16.

JOHN. (*Thinks very hard. Finally:*) Have they?

TROUGHTON. Yes, sir. You don't have two homes, do you?

JOHN. (*Chuckling.*) No.

TROUGHTON. No. (*Chuckling.*) I mean it's not as though Streatham's in the South of France, is it?

JOHN. (*Chuckling.*) No.

TROUGHTON. Oh. So the hospital must have made a mistake then?

JOHN. Yes. Late at night. Very rushed. Understaffed. And the young doctor in Casualty—nice fellow—but English not too hot—maybe got it a bit confused. I probably sounded rather slurred, too, because of the bang on the head. Yes. (*Slurred.*)25 Kenilworth Avenue, Wimbledon, S.W. 19. He mistakes it for (*Indian voice.*) 47 Lewin Road, Streatham, S.W. 16.

TROUGHTON. (*Bemused.*) Yes.

(*TROUGHTON rises and breaks DR as MARY returns from ULC with Stanley who is wearing a dressing gown over his trousers and slippers.*)

MARY. (*As though announcing an unwelcome guest.*) It's Stanley!

(*STANLEY walks down breezily to DRC. During the following dialogue MARY closes door and comes down to sit on L of John on settee.*)

STANLEY. (*To John.*) You all right, old son?

JOHN. (*Firmly.*) You look bloody awful. (*To Troughton.*) Stanley Gardner. Got the flat upstairs. You're the fuzz, are you?

TROUGHTON. (*Coldly.*) Detective Sergeant Troughton, Wimbledon Police.

STANLEY. (*Smiles at Troughton.*) Jolly good. (*Crosses and sits R of settee. To John.*) Now the milkman told me all about it. Said you'd had a punch-up with half-a-dozen skinheads wielding bicycle chains.

JOHN. I was hit with a handbag if you must know.

STANLEY. Oh, "gay" skinheads, that's new, Sergeant.

TROUGHTON. (*To Stanley.*) Are you a friend of the family, sir?

STANLEY. (*Puts his arm around John's shoulder.*) I most certainly am. I've been borrowing the odd fiver off John for a couple of years now, haven't I?

MARY. Yes, you have!

STANLEY. (*To Troughton.*) Yes, another couple of years I'll start paying it back!

(*STANLEY chuckles at his own joke. TROUGHTON is not amused.*)

STANLEY. (*To John.*) So the milkman's got it wrong has he?

MARY. He was very brave. He got himself a bag on the head saving some poor old lady from two muggers.

STANLEY. You didn't!

JOHN. (*Touching his head.*) There's hardly anything there now.

STANLEY. Never was much. (*To Troughton.*) He's such a harmless old prune normally.

TROUGHTON. (*To Stanley.*) Aren't you going to be late for work, sir?

STANLEY. (*Rises indignantly and moves to Troughton DR.*) Work? I'm one of the Government's vital statistics.

TROUGHTON. Beg pardon?

STANLEY. I'm temporarily unemployed.

TROUGHTON. I see.

STANLEY. Only I'm considering making it permanent.

TROUGHTON. (*Coldly.*) Really.

STANLEY. Yes, the hours are good.

(*TROUGHTON ignores his remark and crosses in front of Stanley to R of settee.*)

TROUGHTON. (*To John.*) Well, I don't have any more questions, sir. You take your wife's advice and rest up for a bit.

STANLEY. Yes, you rest up, John and let the Sergeant get back to his duties. (*To Troughton.*) Do you know, Sergeant, there's a man knocked down in Wimbledon every five minutes.

TROUGHTON. (*Unimpressed.*) Really.

STANLEY. Yes, and he's getting bloody fed up with it!

(*STANLEY laughs at his own joke but TROUGHTON "backs" him to DR where STANLEY sits in the chair.*)

TROUGHTON. (*To Stanley, sternly.*) If there were more people around like your friend here, we'd have a lower crime rate.

STANLEY. Of course.

TROUGHTON. (*To Mary.*) He may have caused you some concern, Mrs. Smith, but like I said, your husband's a hero. I expect you'll have the Press boys on to you.

JOHN. (*Rising.*) Press?

(*MARY "sits" John again.*)

TROUGHTON. And I'll just give you the telephone number of the Station in case you remember anything more about those two villains.

(*TROUGHTON has got out his pen and notebook. MARY rises.*)

TROUGHTON. (*As HE writes.*) You can call me any time. Or speak to one of my men.

MARY. Thank you, Sergeant.

(*During the following three lines of dialogue MARY takes the page from TROUGHTON, which HE has torn from his notebook and puts it by phone on table L end of settee.*)

TROUGHTON. 'Morning then, Mr. Smith. Mrs. Smith.

MARY. I'll see you out.

TROUGHTON. (*To Stanley, coldly.*) 'Morning, sir.

(*TROUGHTON moves to door ULC which MARY has opened for him.*)

STANLEY. (*Genially.*) And don't worry, Sergeant, I don't believe half the stuff I read about you boys in the newspapers.

TROUGHTON. (*Stops and turns by door.*) "Gardner," was it, sir?

STANLEY. Yes, but you can call me "Stanley."

TROUGHTON. (Dead-pan.) I know what I'd call you, sir.

(*TROUGHTON exits ULC followed by MARY who closes door. STANLEY rises happily and moves to John.*)

STANLEY. Well, quite a morning and we haven't even had breakfast yet. (*Takes John's cup of coffee.*) Thanks.

(*As STANLEY moves in front of JOHN drinking coffee, Mary's telephone at L of settee rings. JOHN goes to lift receiver but STANLEY, who is beside it, gets there first. During the early part of the ensuing speech JOHN looks at his watch and decides to go. HE goes to behind settee and puts his jacket on.*)

STANLEY. (*On phone.*) Smith residence ... No I'm not ... Yes he is but he's incapacitated at the moment ... U.P.I. What's that? ... Oh!

(*JOHN is now wondering who Stanley could be talking to so moves DR of settee.*)

JOHN. Who is it?

STANLEY. U.P.I. Sssh! (*On phone.*) Fine ... Yes. Flat A, 25 Kenilworth Avenue, Wimbledon, S.W. 19 ... O.K., bye. (*HE replaces receiver.*) That was U.P.I.

JOHN. What's that mean?

STANLEY. United Press International.

JOHN. Press?

STANLEY. Sort of agency that doles out stuff to all the newspapers.

JOHN. (*Moves to Stanley at L end of settee. Aghast.*) You gave them my address.

STANLEY. Yes, that policeman was right. You're going to be a hero.

JOHN. I won't see them.

STANLEY. Why on earth not? Just an interview. Probably a photograph.

JOHN. (*Grabs Stanley. Hoarsely.*) Photograph?!

(*During the above dialogue MARY has returned from ULC closing door. SHE is making her way to kitchen DL.*)

JOHN. I'm not seeing anybody, Mary. (*Hurries over to Mary at door DL.*)

MARY. What?

STANLEY. The press have just been on the phone. They're sending somebody over.

JOHN. They've got a damn cheek.

MARY. The hospital gave him some tablets. I'll get them. (*SHE exits into kitchen DL.*)

JOHN. (*Shouts after her.*) I'm still not meeting anybody! (*Closes kitchen door.*)

STANLEY. Take it easy, old son. (*Sits John in chair DL.*)

JOHN. (*Rising.*) Stanley, you don't understand.

STANLEY. You're right there. Blimey, when you think of half the rubbish the papers print, you deserve to be on the front page.

JOHN. (*Pulls Stanley away from kitchen to DC.*) Stanley! Nothing must be said about me in the

newspapers. You'll have to deal with them when they get
here. Say it wasn't me, say it was you. Say anything.

STANLEY. What the hell are you talking about?

JOHN. It would ruin me.

STANLEY. If this story appears in the papers?

JOHN. Yes! I'll be ruined with Barbara.

STANLEY. Why should you be ruined—(*HE stops.*)
Who's Barbara?

JOHN. She's—a lady.

STANLEY. A lady? (*HE suddenly realizes.*) Ooo! You
naughty naughty Johnny. So Barbara's a little bit on the
side, is she?

JOHN. There's more to Barbara than that.

STANLEY. She's got a big bit, eh? Lovely!

(*STANLEY indicates a large bosom. JOHN pulls Stanley
down on to the settee. During the next couple of pages
while JOHN tells his story both JOHN and STANLEY
must be aware that Mary is only in the kitchen and
could come in at any moment.*)

JOHN. Stanley! All hell would be let loose if Barbara
were to see anything in the newspapers about me and Mary
and living in Wimbledon.

STANLEY. Why?

JOHN. Because I live with Barbara in Streatham.

STANLEY. No, old son, you live with Mary in
Wimbledon.

JOHN. That, too.

STANLEY. (*Blankly.*) You've got two homes?

JOHN. Yes.

STANLEY. One *here* with Mary—?

JOHN. Yes.

STANLEY. And one with your girl friend in
Streatham?

JOHN. Yes. Only Barbara's not my girl friend.

STANLEY. What is she, a Shetland Pony?

JOHN. She's my wife.

STANLEY. I beg your pardon?

JOHN. Barbara and I are married.

STANLEY. (*Nonplussed.*) Mary and you are married.

JOHN. That too.

STANLEY. (*Staggered.*) You've got two wives?

JOHN. Yes.

STANLEY. And two homes?

JOHN. Yes.

STANLEY. God almighty, I thought you were *ordinary!*

JOHN. Yes.

STANLEY. (*Shakes his head in disbelief.*) I can't believe it.

JOHN. I think I've always been a bit surprised myself.

STANLEY. And you just flit between Wimbledon and Streatham like some over-sexed bumble bee, do you?

JOHN. Sort of.

STANLEY. But, blimey, *Streatham.* That's practically next door.

JOHN. Four and a half minutes in the taxi.

STANLEY. Jeez!

JOHN. It's quite handy actually.

STANLEY. Yes!

JOHN. I mean, driving a taxi's not like an ordinary job, is it? Unusual hours. Morning shift. Afternoon shift. Evening shift. Night shift.

STANLEY. I suppose we should be grateful you're not a Concorde pilot. What about the *expense?* It must cost a fortune.

JOHN. Not really. Both Mary and Barbara work. And then I don't need much pocket money.

STANLEY. No time to spend it.

JOHN. Well, I'm either driving the taxi and rushing back to get to be with Mary or driving the taxi and rushing—

JOHN/STANLEY. (*Together.*) back to get to bed with Barbara.

STANLEY. What do you do on your day off?

JOHN. Sleep a lot.

STANLEY. Yes. (*Gaping at John.*) You did actually *marry* both of them, did you?

JOHN. Oh, yes. Mary was the first. That was three years ago in church. And then I met Barbara four months later.

STANLEY. Four months!?

JOHN. Ssh! She just got into my taxi at Victoria Station. She'd been to Worthing on holiday and we started chatting between Victoria and Streatham where she had this flat. I helped her take her cases up and we chatted some more and she asked me if I'd like a cup of tea. And I said "yes." And we chatted. And then she asked me if I'd like to come to tea the next day and I say "yes" and so I did. And the next day we chatted again—

STANLEY. It's a pity you forgot to mention Mary while you were doing all this bloody chatting.

JOHN. Yes, well one cup of tea lead to another and another and I sort of got carried away, I suppose. And having not mentioned Mary in the first place, I didn't know how to bring it up afterwards.

STANLEY. So you asked Barbara to marry you.

JOHN. No. *She* asked *me*.

STANLEY. (*Rising.*) Gawd Almighty. (*Breaks DRC.*)

JOHN. Well—I didn't have the heart to say "no."

STANLEY. Eh!?

JOHN. So we got married at Streatham Registry Office.

STANLEY. And you moved in with Barbara.

JOHN. Yes.

STANLEY. While still living here with Mary.

JOHN. Yes.

STANLEY. You've committed bigamy, that's what you've done.

JOHN. Well, sort of.

STANLEY. No, not sort of. One hundred percent bigamy.

(*JOHN nods.*)

STANLEY. It a criminal offense.

(*JOHN nods.*)

STANLEY. You could go to jail.

(*JOHN nods.*)

STANLEY. Doesn't that worry you?

JOHN. (*Nods.*) I've been too busy to think about it.

STANLEY. I don't know how you cope.

JOHN. It needs a very tight schedule.

STANLEY. And hell of a stamina. I don't know how you manage it. I can only just about find the energy to satisfy the girl friend and sign on at the Labour Exchange.

JOHN. (*Rises and moves to Stanley.*) Look, I've got to get over to Barbara right away or she'll be worried sick. I'm always bang on time.

STANLEY. I can see why you need that schedule now.

JOHN. I was due back at 7:30 this morning from the Early shift. (*Takes out diary.*)

STANLEY. With Barbara in Streatham.

JOHN. Yes.

STANLEY. (*Takes the diary.*) What are all these letters?

JOHN. Well, I have a sort of code to back up my schedule.

STANLEY. "S.W.M."?

JOHN. Saturday with Mary.

STANLEY. "H.D.B."

JOHN. Half day Barbara.

STANLEY. "L.N.B.E.M.M."

JOHN. Late night Barbara, early morning Mary.

STANLEY. "C.A.T."

JOHN. That's to remind me to take the cat to the vet.

(*MARY returns with bottle of tablets and tumbler of water. JOHN hastily puts the diary away and smiles innocently at Mary.*)

MARY. Here we are, precious. One little table to calm you down.

STANLEY. (*To John.*) In that case you'd better take the whole lot!

(*STANLEY sits DR in chair as JOHN glares at him. During the ensuing dialogue JOHN takes one table and then puts the bottle in his pocket.*)

MARY. Just one (*To John.*) Then it's bed for you, my boy.

JOHN. I can't.

MARY. Yes you can. He's had a shock, hasn't he, Stanley?

STANLEY. I think we all have.

JOHN. (*Glares at Stanley.*) I can't afford to miss a day's business.

MARY. You're in no fit state to be driving.

JOHN. I'll just put in half a day.

MARY. Do you know, Stanley, he's got enough energy for two people.

STANLEY. (*Laughing.*) Yes!

(*Once more JOHN gives Stanley a furious look.*)

MARY. (*To John.*) All right. I'll fix up your lunch box.

(*MARY goes to kitchen door DL. JOHN follows her.*)

JOHN. Don't bother. I want to get back on the road.

MARY. I'm not letting you go without your lunch box.

JOHN. (*Puts his arms around Mary and embraces her.*) You'll make *yourself* late for work.

MARY. I've decided. I won't go into the office today.

JOHN. Won't you?

MARY. (*To Stanley.*) And it's about time you did something about a job, Stanley.

STANLEY. I'm thinking of taking up taxi driving actually.

MARY. Are you?

STANLEY. I'm just beginning to appreciate its attractions.

(*MARY exits into kitchen. JOHN quickly picks up Mary's phone at L of settee and dials.*)

JOHN. (*Whilst dialing.*) Don't be so damn clever. You'll put your foot in it.

STANLEY. Sorry but I'm seeing you through new eyes now. (*Chuckling.*) You randy little devil!

JOHN. Go and keep Mary chatting while I speak to Barbara.

STANLEY. (*Rising.*) Barbara?

JOHN. I can't let her go off to work without knowing I'm O.K.

STANLEY. (*Crosses in front of settee to kitchen door.*) Bloody hell!

JOHN. This business has thrown me right out of gear. Go and make sure Mary doesn't come in.

STANLEY. This is living!

(*STANLEY exits into kitchen as Barbara's phone at R end of settee RINGS. JOHN sits L end of settee. BARBARA hurries in from DR and lifts receiver.*)

BARBARA. (*On phone.*) Hullo?

JOHN. (*On phone.*) Hello, darling.

BARBARA. (*On phone.*) Lovebug, where are you? You're an hour and a half late. (*Sits R end of settee.*)

JOHN. (*On phone, sweetly.*) Sorry my sweet. Taxi broke down.

BARBARA. (*On phone.*) Why didn't you ring earlier?

JOHN. (*On phone, quietly.*) Couldn't get to a phone. I—er took a passenger to Gatwick Airport and conked out half way back.

BARBARA. (*On phone.*) Where are you phoning from now?

JOHN. (*Looks nervously towards kitchen. On phone, quietly.*) I'm—er—in a farmer's cottage. Miles from anywhere. Somewhere off the A23.

BARBARA. (*On phone.*) What's the matter with your voice?

JOHN. (*On phone, quietly.*) I don't want to wake the farmer's wife.

(*STANLEY returns from kitchen and joins John by L end of settee.*)

BARBARA. (*On phone.*) Are you all right? You haven't had an accident, have you?

JOHN. (*On phone.*) No, I'm fine, darling, I'm just a bit sort of flustered.

STANLEY. I say—

JOHN. (*Jumping.*) Ah!

(*BARBARA reacts to the noise in her ear.*)

BARBARA. (*On phone.*) What is it?

JOHN. (*On phone.*) Hang on a second, the *farmer's* just come in.

STANLEY. Farmer?

(*STANLEY looks around for the "farmer." JOHN, still holding telephone, moves to Stanley.*)

JOHN. (*On phone.*) Hang on a second, pumpkin.

STANLEY. (*Laughing.*) Pumpkin!

JOHN. (*To Stanley.*) What do you want?!

STANLEY. I got a message from your number one.

JOHN. What is it?

BARBARA. (*On phone.*) You still there, Johnny?

JOHN. (*On phone.*) Yes, the farmer's just asking me something. (*To Stanley.*) What do you *want?*

STANLEY. Mary says would you like cheese and pickle or eggs and tomato or both.

JOHN. I don't care!

STANLEY. Do you want to check what number two's giving you for dinner first?

(*JOHN glares furiously at STANLEY who grins mischievously.*)

JOHN. One of each! (*Goes to speak on phone again.*)

STANLEY. And a flask of tea or coffee?

JOHN. (*Accidently into phone.*) Coffee!

BARBARA. (*On phone.*) Coffee?

JOHN. (*On phone.*) Sorry, darling. I was speaking to the farmer. He's a bit—er—well, you know what country folk are like.

STANLEY. (*In West Country burr.*) Coffee and sandwiches coming up, Surr.

(*STANLEY goes into kitchen. JOHN moves back to L end of settee.*)

JOHN. (*On phone.*) The farmer was just telling me that the garage has fixed the taxi. I'd better go, my sweet. I wanted to catch you before you left for the office.

BARBARA. (*On phone.*) I'm not going in today.

JOHN. (*On phone, surprised.*) Aren't you?

BARBARA. (*On phone.*) You know I'm not, you're taking the day off, too.

JOHN. Am I? (*Sits L end of settee and hastily looks through his diary.*)

BARBARA. (*On phone.*) It's been planned for ages. Just the two of us. (*Sexily.*) Lazing around.

JOHN. (*On phone, refers to diary.*) Oh, yes, C.D.W.B.

BARBARA. (*On phone.*) "C.D.W.B."?

JOHN. (*On phone.*) Cuddly day with Barbara.

BARBARA. (*On phone.*) Silly boy. You hadn't forgotten about it, had you?

JOHN. (*On phone.*) No. Damn taxi breaking down has thrown me, that's all.

BARBARA. (*On phone.*) Well, you hurry up back home.

JOHN. (*On phone.*) I'm on my way. I'll be four and a half minutes.

BARBARA. (*On phone, surprised.*) Four and a half minutes?

JOHN. (*On phone, realizing.*) Yes. I can cut off the A23 on to the M23 and be in Streatham in a flash. Say ten minutes.

BARBARA. (*On phone.*) You drive carefully. I want you all in one big piece.

JOHN. (*On phone, foolishly.*) Yes.

BARBARA. (*On phone.*) Are you feeling a little bit sexy?

JOHN. (*Looks anxiously towards the kitchen L. On phone, worried.*) Just a little bit.

(*Mary's DOORBELL goes. JOHN rises and takes a pace up LC.*)

JOHN. (*On phone.*) Hang on, the doorbell's going.
BARBARA. (*On phone.*) So what?

(*JOHN immediately stops and speaks nonchalantly.*)

JOHN. (*On phone.*) Mm? Oh, nothing. It's nothing to do with me. (*Calls off to kitchen.*) Stay where you are, I'll get it. (*On phone.*) O.K., sweetheart, I'm on my way right now. Keep everything warm. 'Bye.

BARBARA. (*On phone, rising.*) Oh, John.

JOHN. (*On phone.*) Yes?

BARBARA. (*On phone.*) You'd better ring the Police at Streatham.

JOHN. (*On phone.*) Police?

BARBARA. (*On phone.*) Or shall I?

JOHN. (*On phone.*) Why should either of us ring the Police?

BARBARA. (*On phone.*) I reported you missing this morning.

JOHN. (*On phone.*) Missing!?

(*Mary's front DOORBELL goes again.*)

JOHN. (*On phone.*) Don't do anything. I'll ring you straight back.

(*In his confusion JOHN lays the phone down on L arm of the settee instead of replacing it.*)

JOHN. (*Calls into kitchen.*) I'll get it!

(*JOHN dashes out into Mary's hall, ULC. MARY comes in from kitchen wiping her hands on a tea towel.*)

BARBARA. (*On phone.*) John? (*Sits on R end of settee.*)

MARY. What's that, darling?

(*STANLEY appears in kitchen doorway as MARY moves up LC looking for John.*)

STANLEY. (*Jokingly.*) Get back into the kitchen, woman!

MARY. Thought I heard John call out. (*Sees phone off hook.*) Oh.

(*To Stanley's dismay SHE lifts the receiver. During the next couple of lines STANLEY moves to Mary's L.*)

MARY. (*On phone.*) Hello?
BARBARA. (*On phone.*) Hello?
MARY. (*On phone.*) Were you talking?

BARBARA. (*On phone.*) Yes, it's all right. I'm hanging on for him.

MARY. (*On phone.*) Hanging on for *Who?*

(*STANLEY takes the phone from Mary.*)

STANLEY. Me!

(*BARBARA, rather annoyed, rises and breaks DR.*)

BARBARA. (*On phone.*) My husband!

STANLEY. (*To Mary.*) Damn nuisance not having my own phone upstairs. John said it would be O.K. It's about a job.

(*STANLEY crosses in front of Mary and moves D.C. MARY follows him, interestedly.*)

MARY. (*Bemused.*) Oh. Good.

STANLEY. (*On phone.*) Hello!

BARBARA. (*On phone.*) Hello?

STANLEY. (*On phone.*) Thanks for holding on. Stanley Gardner here.

BARBARA. (*On phone.*) Are you the farmer?

STANLEY. (*On phone, cheerfully.*) Yes, yes. that's right— (*In West country.*) me dear! (*Smiles at Mary who is now standing beside him on his L. On phone.*) You wanted to talk to me, I believe.

BARBARA. (*On phone.*) No, I don't think so.

STANLEY. (*On phone.*) Yes, well, fire away. I'm open to offers.

BARBARA. (*On phone.*) I beg your pardon?

STANLEY. (*To Mary.*) Don't let the coffee boil over.

MARY. (*Not moving.*) No.

(*STANLEY "edges" Mary, who is rather bemused, toward the kitchen.*)

BARBARA. (*On phone.*) Mr. Gardner?! Hello?

STANLEY. (*Is pushing Mary and smiling at her. On phone.*) Yes—I'm interested—yes—very interested.

BARBARA. (*On phone.*) Interested in what?

STANLEY. In–er–it. (*Mary has gone into the kitchen and STANLEY quickly closes kitchen door. On phone.*) Sorry about that. Can Mr. Smith ring you back?

BARBARA. (*On phone.*) I'd rather hang on, if you don't mind. Mr. Smith *is* all right, isn't he?

STANLEY. (*On phone.*) Yes. He was a bit concussed, that's all.

BARBARA. (*On phone.*) Concussed?

STANLEY. (*On phone.*) He's fine now. The country air's doing him good.

BARBARA. (*Moves in to R end of settee. On phone.*) What happened? John didn't say he was hurt.

STANLEY. (*On phone.*) Oh, didn't he?

BARBARA. (*On phone.*) He said the taxi broke down.

STANLEY. (*On phone.*) Yes, it did.

BARBARA. (*On phone.*) Well, how did he get concussed?

STANLEY. (*On phone.*) He bumped his head.

BARBARA. (*On phone.*) His head?

STANLEY. (*On phone.*) On one of our low beams.

BARBARA. (*Sits R end of settee. On phone.*) No!

STANLEY. (*On phone.*) Yes. I'm afraid they're solid sixteenth century oak.

JOHN. (*Hurries in from hall ULC. HE moves UR behind settee and DR.*) It's that damn newspaper man! (*Crosses in front of settee to Stanley at LC.*)

STANLEY. (*Holds out phone.*) Will you deal with this?

(*JOHN takes phone from Stanley and pushes him ULC towards Mary's hall.*)

BARBARA. (*On phone. Rising.*) Hello? (*Angrily breaks DR.*)

JOHN. (*To Stanley.*) United Press International. Get rid of him for me, will you?

(*STANLEY hurries into hall ULC. JOHN closes door and moves DLC to below chair at D.*)

BARBARA. (*Oh phone.*) Hello!?

JOHN. (*On phone, quietly.*) Hello, darling, I thought I'd put you down.

BARBARA. (*On phone.*) John, are you hurt?

JOHN. (*On phone.*) Hurt?

BARBARA. (*On phone.*) Your head.

JOHN. (*On phone.*) Oh, yes.

BARBARA. (*On phone.*) The farmer said you'd banged it on one of his beams.

JOHN. (*On phone, through gritted teeth.*) The farmer should keep his bloody trap shut!

BARBARA. (*On phone.*) Shall I come over to Mr. Gardner's farm and collect you?

JOHN. (*On phone.*) No! No, I'm fine. What were you saying just now about the police?

MARY. (*Comes in from kitchen DL with coffee flask and sandwich box. SHE closes door and stops on John's L.*) There we are!

BARBARA. (*On phone.*) I spoke to Streatham Police.

JOHN. (*Looks at Mary for a second. On phone, pleasantly.*) If you'll hang on I'll get the farmer for you.

BARBARA. (*On phone.*) I don't *want* the farmer!

JOHN. (*On phone.*) Fine, fine. Mr. Gardner will be with you in a second.

(*JOHN smiles at Mary. BARBARA moves angrily towards settee and sits at R. end.*)

BARBARA. (*On phone.*) John?!

MARY. Is that Stanley's call?

JOHN. (*Backs towards the settee.*) Er—yes.

MARY. About a job?

JOHN. Er—yes.

MARY. You said something about a farmer.

JOHN. Er—yes. It's a lady who owns a farm. She thinks Stanley's looking for a job as a farmer.

MARY. (*Laughing.*) A farmer?

JOHN. (*Laughing.*) Yes.

MARY. Why?

JOHN. (*Stops laughing.*) Well, his name's Gardner and she thinks he's a market gardener. (*HE tails off weakly.*) She's got it a bit confused.

BARBARA. (*On phone.*) Are you there?!

JOHN. (*On phone.*) He won't be a moment. I think he could be interested if he doesn't have to start too early in the mornings.

BARBARA. What?!

(*STANLEY and a large newspaper REPORTER [carrying his camera] come in from hall. STANLEY is struggling to keep him out.*)

STANLEY. An Englishman's home is his castle!

REPORTER. I'm just doing my job, mate! I want a picture.

BARBARA. (*On phone.*) John!

JOHN. (*To Reporter.*) Clear off!

BARBARA. (*On phone.*) Clear off!?

JOHN. (*On phone, sweetly.*) Clear the line a minute.

STANLEY. (*To Reporter.*) He doesn't want any publicity! I told you!

REPORTER. And I'm telling you, news is news. (*To Mary.*) Are you Mrs. Smith?

MARY/BARBARA. (*Together.*) Yes./(*On phone.*) John!

JOHN. (*On phone.*) The farmer's on his way.

BARBARA. What!

REPORTER. Get in close to your husband, please. (*Pushes Mary to John's side.*)

JOHN. No!

(*JOHN immediately dives head first into the sofa to hide his face. At the same time HE throws the phone in the air which STANLEY catches.*)

JOHN. (*Yells.*) Ohh, my head!!

(*HE sits on the floor holding his head. MARY rushes to him and takes him in her arms.*)

MARY. Darling!

BARBARA. (*On phone.*) John, are you there?!

REPORTER. Hey!

(*JOHN and MARY look up.*)

REPORTER. Lovely! (*Takes a "flash" shot.*)

JOHN. Hey!

REPORTER. It should make the first edition of the Evening Standard.

JOHN. It bloody well won't.

(*JOHN jumps up and the REPORTER runs out. JOHN rushes out after him.*)

MARY. John!

(*MARY dashes out after John. The voices of JOHN, the REPORTER and MARY are heard shouting as THEY run into the distance. After a moment of silence STANLEY speaks into telephone.*)

STANLEY. (*On phone, brightly.*) The farmer speaking.

BARBARA. (*On phone.*) Where's my husband?

STANLEY. (*On phone.*) Spending a penny.

BARBARA. (*On phone, firmly.*) Has he had an accident?

STANLEY. (*On phone.*) No, I'm sure he made it in time. Look, I must go now, the cows need milking. (*Moo!*)

BARBARA. (*On phone.*) Mr. Gardner, I want to speak to my husband, please.

STANLEY. (*On phone.*) You'll have to shout, our privvy's at the other end of the barley field.

BARBARA. (*On phone, angrily.*) Well tell him to ring me straight back.

STANLEY. (*On phone.*) Hang on a second. I'll get something to write with. (*Picks up the piece of paper [on which Mary has earlier written Troughton's number.]*)

BARBARA. (*On phone.*) He *knows* the number!

STANLEY. (*On phone.*) Yes?

BARBARA. (*On phone, tersely.*) 674-3105.

STANLEY. (*Takes pen from drawer and writes the number on the opposite side of the paper which has Troughton's number. On phone.*) 674-3105.

BARBARA. (*On phone.*) That's 01 from where you are.

STANLEY. (*On phone.*) No, it's not.

BARBARA. (*On phone.*) From outside London.

STANLEY. (*On phone, quickly.*) Yes it is! (*Leaves the page on the table, L of settee.*)

BARBARA. (*On phone.*) I'd like him to ring me back right away.

STANLEY. (*On phone.*) Yes, well of course, he may have spent his penny and driven straight off.

BARBARA. (*On phone.*) Well I want to know what to do about the police.

STANLEY. (*On phone.*) Police?

BARBARA. (*On phone.*) I suppose I'd better ring them and say he's all right.

STANLEY. (*On phone.*) No, don't do anything.

(*Barbara's front DOORBELL goes.*)

BARBARA. (*On phone.*) I must go.

STANLEY. (*On phone.*) Don't go anywhere!

BARBARA. (*On phone.*) What *is* it?

MARY. (*Hurries back in from hall.*) Stanley!

STANLEY. (*On phone.*) Bye, bye. I think some of our chickens are coming home to roost.

(*STANLEY replaces the receiver. During the next few lines, BARBARA hesitates and then exits into her hall to answer her bell.*)

MARY. He hit him!

STANLEY. What? That reporter hit John?

MARY. No. John hit him.

STANLEY. Where's John now?

MARY. I don't know. He got in his taxi and drove off.

STANLEY. Blimey!

MARY. I hope he's not chasing that poor reporter.

STANLEY. No, he's probably gone round—(*Was going to say "to Barbara" but stops.*)

MARY. Round where?

STANLEY. Round the bend.

MARY. I'll get dressed first, then I'll sort John out.

(*MARY hurries into bedroom. STANLEY picks up the piece of paper and quickly checks the number [Barbara's] he'd written earlier. HE then dials as BARBARA returns from her hall with DETECTIVE SERGEANT PORTERHOUSE. Porterhouse is in plain clothes.*)

PORTERHOUSE. I'm sorry if I've called at an inopportune moment, Mrs. Smith.

BARBARA. Quite all right. Is it about my husband?

PORTERHOUSE. Yes it is. You spoke to me earlier at Streatham Police. Detective Sergeant Porterhouse.

(*Barbara's phone goes.*)

BARBARA. Excuse me.

PORTERHOUSE. Of course.

BARBARA. (*Lifts receiver.–To Porterhouse.*) Sit down, will you? (*Indicates chair DR.*)

STANLEY. Thank you.

(*PORTERHOUSE and STANLEY sit at the same time.*)

BARBARA. (*On phone.*) Hello?

STANLEY. (*On phone.*) It's me again—the farmer.

BARBARA. (*On phone, coolly.*) Oh?!

STANLEY. (*On phone.*) I've got to be quick because the pig's in foal.

BARBARA. (*On phone.*) I want to speak with Mr. Smith.

STANLEY. (*On phone.*) He'll be with you any minute so whatever you do, don't contact the police.

BARBARA. (*On phone.*) There's a police sergeant here now.

STANLEY. (*On phone.*) What?!

(*MARY, now wearing a summer dress, enters from bedroom unseen by Stanley.*)

STANLEY. (*On phone.*) Tell the police it's O.K.
MARY. Police?

(*STANLEY turns, startled as MARY moves to him at LC.*)

STANLEY. (*On phone.*) Thank you very much but I'm not interested in joining the police force.

BARBARA/MARY. (*On phone.*) Police force? Police force?

STANLEY. (*On phone.*) No, if the farming job's still vacant, I'd rather go for that. (*HE puts the phone down, to Mary.*) Bloody labour exchange. I ask you, a policeman.

BARBARA. (*On phone.*) Hello!

MARY. Right, I'm going to find John. I reckon that bang on the head's done more damage than we realized. (*Hurries out into her hall ULC.*)

STANLEY. (*Shouting.*) Mary!

(*STANLEY hurries out after Mary ULC as JOHN enters URC from Barbara's hall obviously having rushed there. HE stands in doorway, panting. BARBARA replaces receiver.*)

PORTERHOUSE. Anything the matter, Mrs. Smith?
BARBARA. No, I don't think so.

PORTERHOUSE. Now, you spoke to me earlier concerning your husband and we've done a check on all the nearby hospitals—

BARBARA. It's all right. I've contacted him.

PORTERHOUSE. Oh good, but there's still one or two things I'd like straightened out.

JOHN. (*Walks down with false nonchalance behind settee to DL.*) Hello, darling!

BARBARA. (*Amazed.*) Sweetheart! (*Hurries over to John and embraces him.*)

JOHN. Sorry I'm a bit late.

BARBARA. How on earth did you get here so quickly?

JOHN. No traffic.

BARBARA. Darling, your head!

JOHN. (*Chuckling.*) It's nothing.

BARBARA. John, this gentleman's from Streatham Police.

JOHN. (*Stops chuckling.*) Streatham Police?

PORTERHOUSE. Detective Sergeant Porterhouse.

JOHN. (*Crosses in front of settee to Porterhouse at DRC.*) Jolly good. Well, I'm back now, safe and sound. Fit as a fiddle. Thanks for calling.

PORTERHOUSE. If I could just clarify a couple of points, sir.

JOHN. (*Backs away and sits C of settee.*) Well, I'm not feeling too good, actually. Banged the old head, you know.

PORTERHOUSE. Yes. Handbag, wasn't it?

BARBARA. Handbag.

JOHN. (*Hesitates.*) Handbag?

PORTERHOUSE. (*Steps in to R. end of settee. Refers to notes.*) John Smith, Casualty Department, Wimbledon Hospital. Concussion and bruising. Cause of damage, lady's handbag.

BARBARA. (*Moves in and sits L of settee.*) Johnny!

(*JOHN looks blankly at Barbara. HE then looks closely at Porterhouse's notebook.*)

JOHN. (*Finally.*) What a coincidence!

PORTERHOUSE. Coincidence, sir?

JOHN. Two John Smiths. Both getting their heads bashed. On the same day.

BARBARA. This one's not you, then?

JOHN. No. Mind you. "John Smith" – common name. (*Refers to Porterhouse's notes.*) Well, you can see it's not me. This fellow got involved with an old lady, two muggers and a handbag. I banged my head on an old oak beam.

PORTERHOUSE. So you weren't in Wimbledon in the early hours of this morning—

JOHN. (*Broadly.*) No.

PORTERHOUSE. —driving your taxi?

JOHN. (*Goes to say "no" but stops.*) Taxi?

PORTERHOUSE. (*Refers to notes.*) Says here this bloke's occupation is a taxi driver.

BARBARA. No!

JOHN. (*Looks blankly at Barbara, then looks at notes and once again "studies" them. With amazement:*) What a coincidence! (*Suddenly.*) Ah!

PORTERHOUSE. What, sir?

JOHN. According to your notes, this Mr. Smith was released from Wimbledon Hospital at 8:30 a.m. this morning.

PORTERHOUSE. That's right.

JOHN. Couldn't be me then. I was in the country at that time. I rang you, didn't I, darling, from the farm.

BARBARA. Yes, there's something peculiar about that farm though.

(*JOHN rises with BARBARA and breaks DLC.*)

JOHN. Yes. It was a bit of a funny farm. (*To Porterhouse.*) Well, thanks for going to all this trouble, Sergeant.

PORTERHOUSE. There is something else, sir.

JOHN. Ye-es? (*Smiles at Barbara and puts his arm around her.*)

PORTERHOUSE. Our colleagues in the Wimbledon force took this *other* Mr. Smith home to an address in Wimbledon.

JOHN. He probably lives in Wimbledon.

PORTERHOUSE. Yes, but somehow or other, the hospital have his address in their records as 47 Lewin Road, Streatham, S.W. 16.

(*JOHN looks suitably "astonished."*)

BARBARA. That's our address, John!

(*JOHN walks over to Porterhouse and "studies" Porterhouse's notes.*)

JOHN. (*Amazed.*) Now, that *is* a coincidence.

PORTERHOUSE. That's what *I* thought.

JOHN. Of course!

PORTERHOUSE. Yes, sir?

JOHN. (*Thinking madly.*) The reason Wimbledon Hospital has this other John Smith's address as mine here is because—I was in the hospital a couple of days ago and they've got their records confused.

(*PORTERHOUSE takes this in.*)

BARBARA. You didn't mention it, pumpkin.

JOHN. (*Moves to Barbara.*) Well, it wasn't serious, pumpkin. I just nipped into their casualty department. (*To Porterhouse.*) Banged my head under the taxi bonnet, checking the plugs.

PORTERHOUSE. You're dead unlucky with your head, aren't you?

JOHN. (*Moves back to Porterhouse.*) Yes. I'm always doing it. I was in and out of the place in five minutes. It was nothing. But, of course, they took down all my particulars. (*To Porterhouse.*) That explains it, doesn't it?

PORTERHOUSE. Does it?

(*JOHN refers through the ensuing speech to Porterhouse's notes as though the information was obvious.*)

JOHN. (*Smoothly.*) Yes, the hospital has both my address from the other day and the address of the *other* Mr. Smith—from this morning. Naturally, the *other* Mr. Smith asks the police to take him to an address in Wimbledon—where he lives—but when the hospital is asked for the other Mr. Smith's address they look up the wrong page in their casualty book and see John Smith, Taxi Driver, Nature of Injury— abrasion of the cranium— and give you my address in Streatham—not realizing that on the very next page is the address of the other John Smith, Taxi Driver, Nature of Injury—abrasion of the cranium—who's just gone home to Wimbledon.

PORTERHOUSE. (*Looks totally blank for a moment. Finally:*) Well, I think that explains it all then.

JOHN. Yes! You can close the file!

(*JOHN escorts Porterhouse to door URC. BARBARA hurries up and opens door.*)

BARBARA. I'm sorry I put you to all this trouble, Sergeant.

PORTERHOUSE. Quite all right, madam.

BARBARA. I'll see you out.

PORTERHOUSE. Thank you. (*To John.*) Oh, by the way, sir. Your head.

JOHN. Yes?

PORTERHOUSE. Where did you have the injury treated?

JOHN. Ah. Do you mean the taxi bonnet bashing or the oak beam bashing?

PORTERHOUSE. The beam, sir. Your most *recent* misfortune. Which hospital treated that?

JOHN. They didn't. No. The farmer's wife is an ex-nurse and she fixed it.

PORTERHOUSE. Ex-nurse, eh?

JOHN. Yes. I always seems to fall on my feet.

PORTERHOUSE. Good. I hope you always check what you've landed in.

(*PORTERHOUSE smiles politely and exits into Barbara's hall, followed by BARBARA. JOHN breathes a sigh of relief and sits in chair DR, studying his diary as MARY and STANLEY enter ULC from Mary's hall. Stanley is still in dressing gown.*)

MARY. He really shouldn't be driving, Stanley. I should have put my foot down.

STANLEY. He'll be all right.

MARY. I'm going to ring that Sergeant Troughton at Wimbledon Police.

STANLEY. I don't think you should do that.

MARY. He wrote his number here somewhere. Yes. (*SHE picks up the piece of paper from the table L of settee.*) Said we could speak to him or one of his men.

(*Dials the number which happens to be Barbara's instead of Troughton's.*)

STANLEY. John will be very upset if you involve the police.

MARY. I'm just worried what he might go and do. They should have kept him in hospital for observation.

STANLEY. I'm with you there.

(*Barbara's phone RINGS. JOHN rises and picks it up.*

JOHN. (*On phone, breezily.*) Yep?
MARY. (*On phone.*) Hello, it's Mary Smith speaking.

(*For a moment John's mind goes completely blank. HE then blinks, takes the phone from his ear and looks at it. HE then puts the receiver back to his ear.*)

MARY. (*On phone.*) Hello, is that Wimbledon Police Station?

(*JOHN's mind is a whirl.*)

MARY. (*On phone.*) Hello!
STANLEY. (*To Mary.*) What's up?
MARY. Don't know. Someone answered and now all I can hear is heavy breathing. (*On phone.*) Hello!

(*JOHN still can't think what to do.
STANLEY takes the phone from Mary.*)

STANLEY. (*On phone.*) Hello! Stanley Gardner here.

(*JOHN is now totally bemused.*)

STANLEY. (*On phone.*) Hello!! (*HE listens. To Mary.*) Well, they're still breathing, anyway. (*Hands the phone back to Mary.*)

MARY. (*On phone.*) Anybody there?

(*JOHN is totally bewildered. STANLEY has been idly looking at the piece of paper which HE has taken from Mary.*)

STANLEY. (*Suddenly.*) Mary—which of these two numbers did you dial?

MARY. That one. 674-3105.

STANLEY. Allow me!

(*HE quickly takes the phone from Mary and moves in front of her to DC. MARY follows him.*)

STANLEY. (*On phone.*) Hello! Stanley Gardner here. Come in Wimbledon! Gardner to Wimbledon, May day, May day, May day!!

(*JOHN is utterly confused and moves DR.*)

JOHN. (*On phone, hoarsely.*) What the hell's going on?

STANLEY. (*On phone.*) Ah, there you are, Wimbledon! (*To Mary.*) Trouble on the switchboard. (*On phone.*) Can I speak to one of the men?

JOHN. (*On phone.*) Men?

STANLEY. (*On phone.*) Or the Sergeant if he's there.

JOHN. (*On phone.*) Have you flipped your bloody lid?!

STANLEY. (*On phone, cheerfully.*) No, no. Nothing like that. (*To Mary.*) He's putting me through to one of the men. (*On phone.*) Hello, Constable!

JOHN. (*On phone.*) Constable?! What in God's name are you playing at Stanley?!

STANLEY. (*On phone.*) I'm speaking on behalf of Mrs. Smith. (*Pointedly.*) She's concerned about her husband's *behavior.*

JOHN. (*On phone.*) How the blazes did you get this number?

MARY. (*To Stanley.*) Let *me* talk to him! (*SHE moves in front of Stanley and grabs the phone from him. SHE is now next to John. On phone.*) Hello, Constable!

(*JOHN's mind whirls once more.*)

MARY. (*On phone.*) Will somebody get Sergeant Troughton for me, please?

(*Behind them Detective Sergeant TROUGHTON comes through Mary's hall door ULC. HE walks down into the lounge. STANLEY sees Troughton. For a brief second HE is dumbstruck. Then HE indicates for Troughton to be silent and calmly escorts Troughton into kitchen DL. All this has been unseen by Mary. SHE turns to where Stanley has been standing.*)

MARY. This is absolutely rid— (*SHE stops on seeing Stanley no longer there. Calls:*) Stanley? (*SHE goes back to the telephone. On phone.*) Hello!

(*JOHN gently replaces the receiver. MARY reacts and then dials again purposefully. JOHN is gently replacing his telephone on the table R of settee as BARBARA enters behind him.*)

BARBARA. (*Brightly.*) Darling!
JOHN. Ah! (*In his fright bangs the telephone down on the table.*)
BARBARA. (*Surprised.*) All right, Precious?

JOHN. You bet. Can't stay, though. (*Looks at telephone, still madly thinking.*)

BARBARA. Can't stay?

JOHN. No. Got to get back on the road. (*HE moves to go.*)

BARBARA. Don't be silly! It's. C.D.W.B.

JOHN. Oh, yes,

BARBARA. (*Puts her arms 'round him and kisses his neck.*) "Cuddly day with Barbara."

JOHN. No, "Can't Do What's Booked."

(*Barbara's phone RINGS. JOHN lifts phone, does a few very quick "heavy breathings" into receiver and replaces receiver. MARY reacts then bangs her phone down and exits into her hall.*

BARBARA looks bewildered at JOHN who is standing, looking at the phone with a blank stare.)

BARBARA. (*Finally.*) Why did you do that?

JOHN. (*For a moment doesn't answer. –Sexily.*) I don't want us to be disturbed.

BARBARA. (*Sexily.*) Oh, you're in a hurry, are you?

JOHN. (*Glancing at phone.*) Not half! But I can't give in to it.

BARBARA. (*Wrapping herself around him.*) Yes, you can.

JOHN. No. You see, I didn't earn a penny last night. I ought to do one quick trip.

BARBARA. Afterwards. (*SHE removes his jacket and during the ensuing dialogue undoes his shirt.*)

JOHN. Well, I've got a bit of a headache, actually.

BARBARA. That's all the more reason for going to bed.

JOHN. I don't think that'll be good for me, honestly. I don't.

BARBARA. You've always said it cures anything.

JOHN. Well, yes.

BARBARA. Especially headaches.

JOHN. Yes, that's *your* headaches, not *my* headaches.

BARBARA. Come on. (*SHE pulls him towards the bedroom DR.*) We'll soon get rid of that nasty old headache.

JOHN. Well, as long as you let me go out afterwards.

(*SHE drags him into bedroom as STANLEY comes out of Mary's kitchen, followed by TROUGHTON.*)

STANLEY. (*Looks around.*) Yes, well, I thought I ought to explain, Sergeant.

TROUGHTON. Dreadful bit of news.

STANLEY. You walked right in the middle of the phone call, you see. Mrs. Smith was shattered.

TROUGHTON. Bound to be. I'm glad you told me.

STANLEY. Yes. Always worse when you hear suddenly like that.

TROUGHTON. Yes. *Both* her grandparents, was it?

STANLEY. Yes, both.

TROUGHTON. Dear oh dear!

STANLEY. Yes, dear, oh dear.

TROUGHTON. On a hiking holiday, too.

STANLEY. Yes. Both in their eighties, mind you.

TROUGHTON. Still, not a nice way to go—over the side of a mountain.

STANLEY. It was quick though.

TROUGHTON. Snowdon, you say?

STANLEY. Yes. (*Pulling himself together.*) Now you wanted to see Mr. Smith again, did you?

TROUGHTON. Yes, I did actually. It appears there's some confusion over Mr. Smith's address.

STANLEY. Is there?

TROUGHTON. As to whether it was in Wimbledon or Streatham.

STANLEY. (*Is taken aback.–Off-hand.*) Wimbledon or—er—St—St—

TROUGHTON. Streatham, sir. Mr. Smith reckoned it was all a silly mistake on the part of the hospital.

STANLEY. Probably was.

TROUGHTON. No, it wasn't. When I got back to the Station, they'd had Streatham Police on to say that another John Smith was reported missing from that area.

STANLEY. (*In mock amazement.*) No!

TROUGHTON. 47 Lewin Road, Streatham, S.W. 16.

STANLEY. Good lord.

TROUGHTON. And that's the same address as they had at the hospital.

STANLEY. It's a puzzle, isn't it?

TROUGHTON. So do you know the present whereabouts of *our* Mr. Smith?

STANLEY. No. I think he's on the job at the moment.

TROUGHTON. Driving his taxi, you mean.

STANLEY. Yes.

TROUGHTON. Well, I think I'll go and call on this other Mr. Smith. (*Moves up to door ULC.*)

STANLEY. (*Worried.*) Call on him? (*Hurries after Troughton.*)

TROUGHTON. In Streatham.

STANLEY. (*Worried.*) Do you think you should?

TROUGHTON. It's only in the next Manor.

STANLEY. Outside your jurisdiction though, isn't it?

TROUGHTON. Just a social call, Mr. Gardner, just a social call.

(*TROUGHTON goes out into Mary's hall. STANLEY dashes to Mary's telephone as TROUGHTON returns.*)

TROUGHTON. Oh, Mr. Gardner.

STANLEY. (*Falls backwards over the settee in his surprise but tries to look nonchalant.*) Yes?

TROUGHTON. Do you know what an accessory is?

STANLEY. (*Considers this.*) A handbag?

(*TROUGHTON shakes his head.*)

STANLEY. Oh, an *accessory*. Yes.

TROUGHTON. Good.

(*TROUGHTON exits. STANLEY picks up piece of paper and, whilst dialing goes to hall door to check that Troughton's actually gone.*

Barbara's phone RINGS. After a moment JOHN hurries in from the bedroom and picks up phone. John now wears underpants, socks and shoes. STANLEY sits L of settee waiting impatiently for the phone to be answered.)

JOHN. (*On phone.*) Hello?

STANLEY. (*On phone.*) It's me again—

JOHN. (*On phone.*) What the hell do you want now?! (*Sits R of settee.*)

STANLEY. (*On phone.*) It's no good getting cross with me. I'm just the bloke who's got the flat upstairs!

JOHN. (*On phone.*) Blimey, talk about fiddling while Rome burns.

JOHN. (*On phone.*) Well, come on, what is it?

STANLEY. (*On phone.*) Troughton is on his way to see you!

JOHN. (*On phone.*) Troughton?

STANLEY. (*On phone.*) The policeman who was here this morning!

JOHN. (*On phone, aghast.*) He's coming over to Streatham?

STANLEY. (*On phone.*) To see John Smith!

JOHN. (*On phone.*) Bloody hell!

STANLEY. (*On phone.*) And Mary's rushed out looking for you!

(*BARBARA appears at bedroom door. She is still in her negligee.*)

BARBARA/JOHN. (*Together.*) Darling—

JOHN. (*On phone, quickly but smoothly.*) Well, thanks for telling me and if I hear of anybody who's looking for that much cucumber I'll put them in touch.

(*HE replaces phone and moves to Barbara. STANLEY looks perplexed.*)

STANLEY. Cucumber?!

JOHN. (*To Barbara.*) I ask you. Two and a half acres of cucumber.

BARBARA. Not that wretched farmer again?

STANLEY. (*On phone.*) Hello? John? (*Gets the piece of paper again, checks and dials number.*)

BARBARA. (*To John.*) Come on beddy-byes.

JOHN. (*Firmly.*) No. I've decided. I'm taking you out!

BARBARA. Out?

JOHN. Yes, why not? We'll have lunch in our little bistro, bottle of wine and then back here to spend the afternoon in bed.

BARBARA. I'm ready for bed *now*.

JOHN. (*Foolishly.*) No. Let's tease ourselves a bit. (*Hurries into bedroom.*)

BARBARA. Darling! (*Starts to run after him as her phone RINGS. SHE grabs it. On phone.*) Hello?!

STANLEY. (*On phone.*) It's Mr. Farmer again, the gardener.

(BARBARA reacts. So does STANLEY.)

BARBARA. *(On phone.)* Look, I doubt very much if my husband will be able to help you. Cucumber just isn't his line.

STANLEY. *(On phone.)* No. It's potatoes actually, this time—

BARBARA. *(On phone.)* We don't want any potatoes!

STANLEY. *(On phone.)* But they're King Edwards—

BARBARA. *(On phone.)* I don't care whose they are, he's not into agriculture. Now, he's very grateful to you for helping him this morning but he's extremely busy.

STANLEY. *(On phone.)* Yes, I'm sure he's got his hands full but it won't take a second.

(JOHN comes out of bedroom tucking his shirt into his trousers. HE's carrying Barbara's dress and shoes.)

JOHN. *(To Barbara.)* Come on, darling, quickly.

BARBARA. What about this wretched farmer?

STANLEY/JOHN. *(On phone. Together.)* Hello?

JOHN. *(To Barbara.)* Has he rung again? You hurry up and get dressed.

(JOHN grabs the telephone and gives Barbara her clothes. HE pushes Barbara towards bedroom.)

JOHN. *(On phone for Barbara's benefit.)* You really must stop ringing me up, Mr. Gardner!

STANLEY. *(On phone.)* It's about Mary!

JOHN. *(On phone, for Barbara's benefit.)* Oh, your Jersey cow, yes I remember.

BARBARA. *(Surprised.)* Jersey cow!

(JOHN neatly eases Barbara into bedroom and closes door.)

JOHN. *(On phone.)* Look, I'm trying to get out before Troughton turns up!

STANLEY. *(On phone.)* I'm worried about Mary.

JOHN. *(On phone.)* I'm worried about *everything*.

STANLEY. *(On phone.)* She's rushed out of the house looking for you.

JOHN. *(On phone.)* I can't do anything about that, can I?

STANLEY. *(On phone.)* But she might have gone round to Wimbledon Police Station to see Sergeant Troughton.

(BARBARA enters from bedroom putting on her dress. SHE is carrying her shoes. During the ensuing dialogue SHE sits in chair DR and finishes dressing.)

JOHN. *(On phone, for Barbara's benefit.)* Yes, well cows are funny animals, aren't they?

STANLEY. *(On phone.)* Eh?

BARBARA. *(To John.)* What's he going on about now?

JOHN. It's all right.

STANLEY. *(On phone.)* Wimbledon Police may tell Mary that Troughton's on his way to see you in Streatham.

JOHN. *(On phone, lightly.)* Yes, well, that would really put the bull among the cows, wouldn't it? I'm rushing out now so I can't really discuss it any further. Naturally, anything you can do to keep the bull and cow apart, you do it!

STANLEY. *(On phone.)* I'll get dressed then see if I can find Mary.

JOHN. (*On phone.*) Thank you. In the meantime just keep a very close watch on your bullocks.

(*STANLEY reacts as JOHN replaces his receiver. STANLEY replaces receiver and hurries out into hall ULC.*)

BARBARA. (*To John.*) What was all that about?
JOHN. He's in a right state. All the Staffordshire Bulls are having a go at his Jersey cow. (*Hastily.*) Right, let's go.

(*During the following speech HE puts on his jacket, which Barbara has removed earlier and thrown on settee.*)

JOHN. We'll have a nice long lunch, bottle of wine then back here to spend the afternoon in bed.

(*HE takes Barbara to hall door URC but stops. HE opens door and, as HE does, Barbara's DOORBELL goes. JOHN immediately shuts the door and marches Barbara away from it to DRC.*)

BARBARA. What's the matter?
JOHN. It—er—might be the police again.
BARBARA. Well, that's all right, isn't it?
JOHN. Different policeman, I mean.

(*The DOORBELL rings again.*)

JOHN. Tell you what, I'll go down the back stairs and meet you outside the bank. (*Moves to kitchen.*)
BARBARA. (*Hurries after him.*) Darling!

JOHN. It it's the police, just confirm what happened to me—er—at the farm and if they want to see me they'll have to make an appointment. (*Opens kitchen door.*)

BARBARA. Are you sure your head's all right?

JOHN. I'm not sure of anything at the moment. I'll see you outside the restaurant. You'll recognize me, I'll be wearing exactly what I'm wearing now.

(*The DOORBELL rings.*
JOHN hurries into kitchen.
BARBARA frowns and goes out URC into her hall as STANLEY returns from Mary's hall ULC. Stanley is now fully dressed.)

STANLEY. (*Calls.*) Mary?! Mary! (*Looks into kitchen.*) Mary?! I sound like a bloody nursery rhyme.

(*STANLEY hurries out into hall ULC as BARBARA returns from the hall URC with BOBBY FRANKLYN. BOBBY is in a bit of a "state."*)

BARBARA. You just caught me, actually.

BOBBY. I'm *so* sorry, lovey.

BARBARA. (*Moves DL towards kitchen.*) It's no trouble, honestly.

BOBBY. (*Moves DR.*) We're just moving in up there and we don't seem to have a *thing* in the flat.

BARBARA. No problem.

BOBBY. (*Crosses to Barbara at DL.*) Although you'd think that dizzy bitch could have remembered to get milk, wouldn't you?

BARBARA. How about sugar and tea?

BOBBY. No, he got those all right. (*Surveying the flat.*) Oh, this is "tres chic."

BARBARA. You short of anything else up there?

BOBBY. Only decorators, darling. We're up to our armpits in paint.

BARBARA. (*Smiling.*) I'm afraid that's not my line.

BOBBY. No, it's not Cyril's either. He won't lift a finger, lazy queen.

BARBARA. I'm Barbara Smith, by the way.

BOBBY. Bobby Franklyn. I'd like to say I won't be a nuisance again but, knowing me, I probably will.

BARBARA. Any time.

BOBBY. For God's sake don't encourage me. I thrive on familiarity.

BARBARA. Well, anything we can do to help. My husband can put his hand to most things.

BOBBY. Can he?!

BARBARA. He's a bit of a handyman.

BOBBY. Well, if he's also young and handsome for God's sake don't let my Cyril get at him.

BARBARA. (*Laughing.*) O.K. Hang on a sec.

BOBBY. Thanks ever so.

(*STANLEY returns from hall ULC as BARBARA exits into her kitchen. BOBBY is looking around Barbara's lounge.*

STANLEY carries the Evening Standard and is looking horrified.)

STANLEY. (*Looks at newspaper.*) Oh, my God! (*Reads.*) "Taxi driver has a go at muggers." Front page— with a picture! I must tell John.

(*STANLEY hurries to phone, picks up piece of paper and dials as BARBARA pops her head around her kitchen door. STANLEY sits L end of settee. BOBBY has wandered to R and is surveying the decor.*)

BARBARA. (*To Bobby.*) I say! Do you and Cyril like home-made cake?

BOBBY. Anything but "fairy."

BARBARA. (*Laughs.*) Chocolate?

BOBBY. Yes! To hell with the corset.

(*HE pats his stomach. BARBARA exits into kitchen. Barbara's telephone RINGS. BOBBY hesitates and then lifts the receiver.*)

BOBBY. (*Brightly.*) Hello!

STANLEY. (*On phone.*) Who's that?

BOBBY. (*Reacts. On phone.*) Bobby Franklyn. I've got the flat upstairs.

STANLEY. (*On phone.*) Well, I hope you're having a better time than I am.

BOBBY. (*On phone.*) I wouldn't know about that. I'll call Mrs. Smith for you.

STANLEY. (*On phone.*) It's *Mr.* Smith I want.

BOBBY. (*On phone.*) He's not in.

STANLEY. (*On phone.*) That's good. At least I think it's good. Did he sort of *rush* out in a state or anything?

BOBBY. (*On phone.*) I don't know *how* he left.

STANLEY. (*On phone.*) No. There aren't any *police* there, are there?

BOBBY. (*On phone.*) Is this a "phone-in" on Capital radio?

STANLEY. (*On phone.*) No.

BOBBY. I'll get Mrs. Smith for you.

STANLEY. (*On phone.*) No. She's probably had enough of me and my King Edwards.

BOBBY. (*Reacts. On phone.*) Well, would you like to leave a message?

STANLEY. (*On phone.*) Er—No. No. Mrs. Smith hasn't got a Standard floating around there has she?

BOBBY. (*On phone.*) A Standard? Floating? (*HE looks in the air for a "flag."*)

STANLEY. (*On phone.*) Newspaper. Evening Standard.

BOBBY. (*On phone.*) Oh. I really wouldn't know. Bit early, isn't it?

STANLEY. (*On phone.*) First edition. (*Quickly.*) She doesn't want to get it, though. It's a dreadful paper.

BOBBY. (*On phone, bemused.*) Yes, all right.

STANLEY. (*On phone.*) Don't you get it either.

BOBBY. (*On phone.*) I won't, I won't. Are you doing some sort of Market Research?

STANLEY. (*On phone.*) No. But if you see Mr. Smith just say Mr. Gardner rang.

BOBBY. (*On phone.*) Gardner.

STANLEY. (*On phone.*) And tell him things aren't too good down on the farm.

(*BARBARA returns from kitchen as STANLEY replaces receiver. During the ensuing dialogue, HE gets pen and pad from table drawer and writes a note, having folded the Evening Standard and put it in his pocket. BARBARA carries a tray on which is a pint of milk and two slices of chocolate cake on plates. SHE moves above settee to BOBBY who is still looking at receiver.*)

BARBARA. Here we are.

BOBBY. Oo, scrummy! I answered your telephone. (*Replaces receiver and takes tray.*)

BARBARA. Thanks. Any message?

BOBBY. Well, King Edward came into it somewhere. And—er—Mr. Gardner.

BARBARA. Oh, *him.*

BOBBY. I couldn't quite make out what he was on about.

BARBARA. He's a damn pest.

BOBBY. Do you get many funny phone calls then?

BARBARA. Only from this fellow. He's trying to get rid of two and a half acres of beetroots.

BOBBY. God help us all! He said to tell Mr. Smith that things weren't too good on the farm.

BARBARA. With him running the place, I'm not surprised. (*Moves up a pace towards door URC.*)

BOBBY. Is Mr. Smith in that line of business then?

BARBARA. No. He drives a taxi.

BOBBY. Oh, lovely. Cyril and I are in the dressmaking caper.

BARBARA. I'll remember that.

BOBBY. Yes. We'll fix you up, love. Evening frock, little afternoon number. The trouble is with Cyril he can't bear to part with half of them! (*HE laughs.*)

BARBARA. (*Laughs and opens door.*) I'll go out with you.

BOBBY. That won't get you anywhere, dear!

(*THEY exit into Barbara's hall URC.*
STANLEY has completed writing his note and is reading it himself as Detective Sergeant PORTERHOUSE walks behind settee to DRC. PORTERHOUSE coughs politely and STANLEY looks up.)

STANLEY. Oh. (*Rises and moves to Porterhouse.*)

PORTERHOUSE. Sorry, sir. All the doors were open.

STANLEY. Oh, were they?

PORTERHOUSE. Detective Sergeant Porterhouse.

STANLEY. (*Worried.*) Ah. Wimbledon Police.

PORTERHOUSE. No. Streatham, actually.

STANLEY. (*Taken aback.*) Streatham?

PORTERHOUSE. Yes. I'm just doing a spot of checking, that's all. Semi-official.

STANLEY. (*Warily.*) Oh, yes?

PORTERHOUSE. Concerning a namesake of yours.

STANLEY. (*Surprised.*) Of mine?

PORTERHOUSE. Bit of a surprise, eh, Mr. Smith?

(*STANLEY goes to speak but stops as he realizes the situation.*)

STANLEY. (*Brightly, but faintly.*) Yes!

PORTERHOUSE. (*Enjoying himself.*) It's all rather a coincidence really. This other Mr. Smith is a taxi-driver too.

STANLEY. (*With mock surprise.*) No!

PORTERHOUSE. Only he lives in Streatham.

STANLEY. No!

PORTERHOUSE. (*Refers to notes.*) John Smith, 47 Lewin Road, Streatham, S.W. 16.

STANLEY. No!

PORTERHOUSE. I've just come from talking to him.

STANLEY. (*Goes to say "No" but:–*) Bloody hell!

PORTERHOUSE. (*Chuckling.*) I thought you'd be surprised!

STANLEY. (*Brightly.*) Yes!

PORTERHOUSE. No, I expect you're wondering what I want from you?

STANLEY. I am rather, yes.

PORTERHOUSE. It's just confirmation, really, of the cause of your head— (*Looks at Stanley's head.*) —injury.

STANLEY. (*Backs to R end settee.*) Oh, yes. I'm a quick healer. It's very tender, mind you.

PORTERHOUSE. (*Moves to Stanley.*) Not surprisingly is it? Must have been quite a blow you received.

STANLEY. They made them solid in the sixteenth century.

PORTERHOUSE. (*Considers this. Frowning.*) Handbags?

STANLEY. (*After a pause.*) Yes, I thought one of policemen said it was antique.

PORTERHOUSE. (*Considers this.*) An antique handbag?

STANLEY. (*Considers this.*) Of course! He was referring to the *woman* when he said I was hit by an old bag.

PORTERHOUSE. (*Takes this in.*) Yes. Well, I think what you say seems to verify—

STANLEY. Does it? Right, if you'll excuse me then, Sergeant I was just about to go to bed.

(*STANLEY moves Porterhouse up R end of settee.*)

PORTERHOUSE. (*Surprised.*) Bed?

STANLEY. Yes, it's—er—Wednesday morning. NWW.

PORTERHOUSE. NWW?

STANLEY. Nooky with wife.

(*STANLEY starts to move Porterhouse behind settee towards hall door as MARY comes in from hall and stops on seeing Porterhouse. For a moment STANLEY is transfixed, but then quickly pulls Porterhouse back out of Mary's sightline. STANLEY hurries to Mary.*)

STANLEY. Hello darling!

(*HE gives Mary a huge kiss and embrace. MARY is suitably surprised. STANLEY pulls her DL away from Porterhouse.*)

STANLEY. (*Flustered.*) Nice to see you back again,Mary. Nothing's happened since you've been gone. Absolutely nothing. I was just leaving you this note, my sweet. There we are.

(*MARY takes the note. During the above, PORTERHOUSE has walked down to R end of settee, interested.*)

MARY. (*Reads it.*) 'Dear Mary. Everything is O.K. Suggest you go to bed for the rest of the day. See you soon. All the very best. Yours, Stanley—
STANLEY. (*Grabbing note. To Porterhouse, quickly.*) Standing room only. (*Chuckles.*) NWW.'

(*HE moves in front of Porterhouse to R and screws up the piece of paper. HE makes a great "show" of throwing it into wastebin by chair DR.*)

STANLEY. (*To Mary.*) Oh, I'm terribly sorry! May I introduce Detective Sergeant—er—
PORTERHOUSE. Porterhouse, Streatham.
STANLEY. Detective Sergeant Porterhouse–Streatham.
PORTERHOUSE. Just Porterhouse. I'm *from* Streatham.
STANLEY. Streatham. Yes. Round the corner.

(*MARY crosses in front of Stanley to Porterhouse so that SHE is now between the two men.*)

MARY. (*To Porterhouse.*) Is it about John?
STANLEY. (*Quickly.*) Yes it is!
MARY. (*Glares at Stanley. To Porterhouse.*) Is John all right?

(*PORTERHOUSE frowns and looks at Stanley who is
    standing the other side of Mary.*)

PORTERHOUSE. Yes, I think so.
STANLEY. Yes, I think so!
MARY. (*Glares at Stanley. To Porterhouse.*) Have you
spoken to him then?
PORTERHOUSE. (*Glances at Stanley.*) Yes, thanks.
STANLEY. Yes, he has!
MARY. (*Glares at Stanley. To Porterhouse.*) When?
PORTERHOUSE. When what?
MARY. (*To Porterhouse.*) When did *you* talk to John?
PORTERHOUSE. (*Surprised.*) Well, just now.
MARY. Just now?
STANLEY. (*Steps in. Quickly.*) Yes, it must have
been. (*To Porterhouse.*) Well, it *was*, wasn't it?

(*MARY pushes Stanley back.*)

PORTERHOUSE. (*Getting confused.*) Yes.
STANLEY. Yes!
MARY. (*Glares at Stanley. To Porterhouse.*) Where?
STANLEY. Where what, dear?!
MARY. (*Glares at Stanley. To Porterhouse.*) Where did
you talk to John?
PORTERHOUSE. (*Glances at Stanley again.*) Well, *I*
was standing here and *he* was standing—
STANLEY. (*Quickly.*) Standing about there!
MARY. (*Glares at Stanley. To Porterhouse.*) I've been
looking everywhere for him.
PORTERHOUSE. (*Surprised, looking at Stanley.*)
Have you?
MARY. (*To Porterhouse.*) Well, where is he now?
PORTERHOUSE. (*Totally confused.*) Who?!
STANLEY. Who'd like a nice cup of tea?

MARY. (*Glares at Stanley. To Porterhouse.*) My husband. Where is he?

(*STANLEY steps in front of Mary and takes Porterhouse DR.*)

STANLEY. (*To Porterhouse.*) Yes, where is he? What's his *position?* Where exactly does he *stand* with the police?

MARY. Stanley!

STANLEY. (*Hesitates a brief second.*) Stanley's gone to school, my sweet.

MARY. (*Tries to fathom this out.*) What?!

STANLEY. Yes, I gave the little chap his cornflakes and saw him on to the bus.

MARY. What's the *matter* with you?

STANLEY. Nothing. I'm fine now, dear. (*To Porterhouse.*) You're happy, too, aren't you?

PORTERHOUSE. Yes, I'm quite satisfied, Mrs. Smith. Now I've talked to him. (*Indicates Stanley.*)

MARY. (*Surprised.*) Him?

STANLEY. Me. Yes. (*To Porterhouse.*) You wanted to talk to me, didn't you? Little chat. It's all O.K. now.

MARY. (*Edgily to Stanley.*) Will you just keep out of this for a moment.

STANLEY. Only trying to help.

MARY. Well, you're not. (*MARY pulls Stanley in front of her and propels him to L end of settee. MARY suddenly notices the newspaper that Stanley has folded and put in his pocket. SHE moves to C.*) Is that the Evening paper?

STANLEY. (*Takes out newspaper.*) Mm? Oh, yes.

MARY. Anything in it about last night's mugging? (*Takes paper.*)

STANLEY. Yes. Front page.

PORTERHOUSE. Front page, eh? You've got a hero for a husband, Mrs. Smith. (*Starts to move to Mary to look at newspaper.*)

MARY. (*Looking at newspaper.*) What a dreadful picture. I look awful. Mind you, John doesn't look too good either.

STANLEY. (*Chuckling.*) No.

(*STANLEY suddenly realizes that the picture shows the "real" John and grabs the paper just as PORTERHOUSE is about to look at it. STANLEY then removes the outside pages from the rest of the newspaper and gives the remainder of the paper to Mary. MARY and PORTERHOUSE look on blankly as STANLEY explains away his action by embarking on a "paper-tearing" routine. HE folds the outside pages several times and then tears various holes in it. HE then unfolds the paper to disclose a row of holes. When HE sees that Mary and Porterhouse are staring at him totally bemused HE crosses in front of them to R. and throws the paper in the wastebin. HE then moves back to C. between Porterhouse and Mary.*)

STANLEY. Now, what were you saying, Sergeant?

MARY. Have you been drinking?

STANLEY. I don't think he said that, did you?

(*PORTERHOUSE dumbly shakes his head. STANLEY moves Mary towards kitchen.*)

STANLEY. But it's a good idea. How about a cup of tea, dear?

MARY. (*Hits Stanley with the newspaper.*) Don't you "dear" me!!

STANLEY. (*To Porterhouse.*) Sorry about this. We've been through a lot this morning.

MARY. Stanley!

STANLEY. Stanley won't be home till after school, dear.

MARY. (*Her nerve is beginning to go.*) What?

STANLEY. Unless they've kept the little chap in again. Naughty Stanley!

MARY. (*Shouting.*) What the *hell* are you talking about?!

(*As SHE shouts, SHE hits Stanley with the newspaper. STANLEY scuttles over to Porterhouse.*)

PORTERHOUSE. (*Nervously.*) No tea for me, thank you.

MARY. (*Not very calmly.*) I'm going to remain quite calm.

STANLEY. (*Takes a pace to Mary.*) That's a very good idea, dear.

MARY. (*Shoves Stanley out of the way and crosses in front of him to Porterhouse. To Porterhouse, anxiously.*) Is there something you're not telling me about John?

PORTERHOUSE. (*Looks at Stanley. Baffled.*) I don't think so, no.

STANLEY. No!

MARY. (*Yells.*) Will you shut up!!

STANLEY. I don't think you should talk to me like that, dear.

MARY. Look, either go upstairs or push off to the labour exchange. (*Pokes Stanley with the newspaper.*)

PORTERHOUSE. (*Politely.*) If you're having a domestic discussion I'll be on my way.

STANLEY. Good idea.

MARY. No! You stay here, please Sergeant. (*To Stanley.*) You – upstairs!

STANLEY. Mary, I've only been trying to—

(*During the ensuing dialogue MARY drags Stanley to the hall door ULC.*)

MARY. Get out!!

STANLEY. I couldn't make a phone call, could I?

MARY. Out!!

STANLEY. Just a quick one.

MARY. (*Beats Stanley about the head with the newspaper. Hysterically:*) If you don't go I'll have you bloody-well evicted!

(*PORTERHOUSE has backed away to the wall at R.*)

STANLEY. (*Hysterically to Porterhouse.*) We play this silly game every Wednesday.

(*It's suddenly all too much for MARY who lets out a wild scream.*)

MARY. Ahhh!

STANLEY. (*Jumping.*) Ahhh!

(*MARY runs DL and collapses in chair as STANLEY rushes out into hall ULC. PORTERHOUSE flattens himself against the wall in fright. For a moment PORTERHOUSE stays transfixed as MARY sits sobbing. Then PORTERHOUSE starts to collect up the newspaper.*)

PORTERHOUSE. (*Trying to be jolly.*) Now, Mrs. Smith, I don't think you should have sent him packing like that. (*Puts newspaper in wastebin DL.*)

MARY. He's a bloody nuisance!

PORTERHOUSE. (*Gives Mary his handkerchief.*) We all have these little rifts. Today's been a bit of a strain. You and he will be all right after a kiss and cuddle.

MARY. (*Is astonished.*) Kiss and cuddle?!

PORTERHOUSE. Never fails. Do what you were planning to do and spend the morning together in bed.

(*MARY rises, outraged and moves in front of Porterhouse to DC.*)

MARY. (*Outraged.*) I was planning no such thing.

PORTERHOUSE. Well *he* was.

(*MARY turns, surprised.*)

MARY. (*Angrily.*) Was he?! Well, I assure you the last thing I'd do is jump into bed with that moron.

PORTERHOUSE. I'm sorry to hear that.

MARY. (*Moves back to chair DL.*) I don't indulge in that sort of thing.

PORTERHOUSE. I'm sorry to hear that, too.

MARY. (*Outraged.*) What sort of wife do you think I am?

PORTERHOUSE. I really don't know.

MARY. Once you start that sort of think you've got no marriage at all.

PORTERHOUSE. (*Surprised.*) Well, it takes all sorts, I suppose.

MARY. Yes.

PORTERHOUSE. I'm surprised that you ended up with little Stanley.

MARY. (*Is now confused.*) I don't intend to end up with "little Stanley."

PORTERHOUSE. (*Worried.*) Oh, dear.

MARY. (*Gives Porterhouse the hanky and sits.*) The way he's been acting this morning, I think the sooner he's put away, the better.

PORTERHOUSE. No, no! The young fellow needs physical love and lots of it.

MARY. What?!

PORTERHOUSE. (*Chuckling.*) I can see my wife could teach you a thing or two.

(*During the following dialogue JOHN appears stealthily from kitchen DL. HE looks around and then moves in front of Mary and Porterhouse to Barbara's door URC to check if Barbara is around. JOHN then moves DRC to Barbara's phone and dials.*)

MARY. (*To Porterhouse.*) If I could just resolve what's happened to my husband.

PORTERHOUSE. As far as I'm concerned, he's clarified the situation.

MARY. But you said you'd seen him and I'd like to know where he is?

PORTERHOUSE. (*Hesitates and looks up.*) Well, he's upstairs, isn't he?

MARY. (*Hesitates and looks up.*) What's John doing up there?

PORTERHOUSE. (*Hesitates and looks up.*) Isn't that where he went?

MARY. (*Hesitates and looks up.*) To see Stanley?

PORTERHOUSE. (*Frowning.*) I thought Stanley was at school?

(*PORTERHOUSE scratches his head, confused.*

Mary's telephone RINGS.
MARY picks it up as PORTERHOUSE sits in chair, DL trying to work it all out.)

MARY. (*On phone.*) Hello?
JOHN. (*Sits R settee. On phone. Relieved.*) Oh thank goodness!
MARY. (*On phone. Furious.*) John! Where are you?!

(PORTERHOUSE looks in the direction of "upstairs" whilst JOHN hesitates for a moment.)

JOHN. (*On phone.*) Never mind that. Is everything all right?
MARY. (*On phone.*) Sort of, yes.
JOHN. (*On phone.*) Nothing awful's happened?
MARY. (*On phone.*) No. There's a policeman here but that's been sorted out.
JOHN. (*On phone.*) A policeman?
MARY. (*On phone.*) From Streatham.
JOHN. (*On phone.*) Oh, yes?
MARY. (*To Porterhouse.*) Do you want to talk to him?
PORTERHOUSE. (*Hesitates and looks up. Puzzled.*) No, thanks.
MARY. (*On phone.*) No, the Sergeant's quite happy, I think.
JOHN. (*On phone.*) Oh, good. Is—er—Stanley about?
MARY. (*On phone.*) I think Stanley's been drinking.

(PORTERHOUSE reacts surprised.)

MARY. (*On phone.*) Or he's on drugs.

(PORTERHOUSE reacts appalled.)

JOHN. (*On phone.*) He's had a lot to contend with this morning, darling.

MARY. (*On phone.*) The sooner he leaves here and shacks up with that girl friend of his, the better.

(*PORTERHOUSE reacts horrified and rises, breaking DL. JOHN rises.*)

JOHN. (*On phone.*) Well, look darling, I'm on my way home right now.

MARY. (*On phone.*) Yes, you hurry up back, sweetheart. Then it's straight to bed.

JOHN. (*On phone.*) Great. I'll be five minutes.

MARY. (*On phone.*) All right. Five minutes.

(*JOHN and MARY blow each other kisses and replace receivers. JOHN hurries out into Barbara's hall. PORTERHOUSE moves to Mary.*)

PORTERHOUSE. I'm pleased that you and your husband have patched it up.

MARY. Patched what up?

PORTERHOUSE. That's it. Don't harbour grudges. That's what's kept me and my Missus together for twenty years. Well, I'll be off then, Mrs. Smith. Don't bother to see me out.

MARY. (*Hurries ULC and opens door.*) I'm sorry if it's been a bit hectic here this morning.

PORTERHOUSE. All in a day's work. And, Mrs. Smith. Little word of advice about Stanley. Just take his trousers down and give him a treatment.

(*PORTERHOUSE exits into Mary's hall ULC. MARY shakes her head in confusion. SHE then exits DL into kitchen as JOHN and BARBARA come in from their*)

*hall URC. BARBARA carries the Evening Standard.
Barbara and John have obviously been having a row.
They come to DC.)*

BARBARA. I felt a right fool!

JOHN. I'm sorry, sweetheart.

BARBARA. I've been standing outside the bank for ten minutes.

JOHN. (*Puts his arms around her and kisses her neck.*) I've said I'm sorry. We must have missed each other. I came back here to look for you.

BARBARA. Honestly!

JOHN. Did—er—you deal with the police?

BARBARA. What police?

JOHN. Just now.

BARBARA. Oh, no. That wasn't the police.

JOHN. (*Worried.*) Wasn't it?

BARBARA. We've got new neighbors upstairs. They wanted some milk.

JOHN. (*Thinking madly.*) You mean, the police haven't been here yet?

BARBARA. Not that I know of. Not since the Sergeant this morning.

JOHN. Oh, dear.

BARBARA. (*Moves towards kitchen.*) Well, I'm going to make some coffee then sit quietly for five minutes and read the paper.

JOHN. (*Moves to her.*) No, don't let's hang around here. After lunch we'll go to bed, read the papers and have a lovely—(*HE suddenly sees front page.*) Ahhh!

BARBARA. What on earth's the matter?

(*JOHN starts to back away to settee.*)

JOHN. What's the matter with what?

BARBARA. You looked at the front page and practically died.

JOHN. Yes.

BARBARA. Something awful's happened, hasn't it?

JOHN. Yes, Mrs. Thatcher's expecting a baby.

BARBARA. That's impossible!

JOHN. That's what Mr. Thatcher says.

BARBARA. Here, let's have a look.

(BARBARA grabs paper towards her. JOHN doesn't let go.)

JOHN. No! *(Pulls paper back towards him.)*

BARBARA. Don't be silly. *(Takes the newspaper.)*

JOHN. *(Grabs the newspaper.)* No, it's my newspaper.

BARBARA. *(Grabs paper.)* Actually, it's mine.

JOHN. *(Grabs paper.)* No. No. I've got it! I *want* it. I *need* it.

(JOHN sits in R corner of settee. HE then rips a "strip" off the front page and, to BARBARA's amazement, HE starts to eat it.)

JOHN. *(Chewing.)* Mm. Very nice.

BARBARA. *(Takes a page back, astonished.)* What in God's name are you doing?

JOHN. *(Munching brightly.)* Eating the newspaper.

BARBARA. For heaven's sake!

(SHE steps in to take the newspaper so HE tears off another strip and pops it in his mouth. BARBARA backs away to DL.)

BARBARA. Darling, it must be something to do with that bang on the head.

BOBBY. (*Enters from hall with tray and clean plates. HE moves DR.*) Door was open! I told you I'd get familiar.

BARBARA. (*Confused.*) That's O.K.

BOBBY. (*To John.*) And you must be this lovely lady's—

(*The words die in his mouth as HE sees that John has a strip of newspaper protruding from his mouth. JOHN quickly gobbles up the strip. BOBBY looks at the torn newspaper in John's hand.*)

BOBBY. Am I interrupting anything?

(*JOHN shakes his head and smiles politely indicating he can't speak with his mouth full.*)

BOBBY. No, that's all right. Don't rush it. Bobby Franklyn from upstairs. How do you do?

(*BOBBY steps forward and holds out his hand but JOHN tears off another strip and pops it into his mouth. BOBBY watches in amazement. JOHN offers Bobby a "piece" to eat and BOBBY shakes his head dumbly.*)

BOBBY. (*Pulling himself together.*) Yes, well—if you're in the middle of eating. (*Crosses in front of settee to Barbara.*)

BARBARA. (*Trying to put on a brave face.*) I'm sorry about this.

BOBBY. No, I'm all for something different. Yes. Oh, thanks for the chocolate cake. (*Gives Barbara the tray but is unable to take his eyes off John.*) Yes. I've er—I've never actually seen anybody eat—er—that *is* newspaper, isn't it?

(*JOHN nods happily. BOBBY starts to move above settee towards door URC.*)

BOBBY. Yes! (*To Barbara.*) Well, I must get back to Cyril. Poor cow's up to his eyes in paint—(*To John.*) Good luck with the diet. (*At door.*) Is that today's? Nice and fresh. (*Exits into hall URC.*)

BARBARA. (*To John.*) What the hell are you *up* to?!

(*JOHN indicates that he can't speak because his mouth is now bulging with chewed newspaper.*)

BARBARA. I'll get you some coffee to wash it down! (*Moves towards the kitchen and stops.*) I don't know what that Mr. Franklyn must think.

JOHN. (*Unintelligible.*) He's queer!

BARBARA. Not half as queer as you are.

(*BARBARA exits into kitchen. JOHN heaves a sigh of relief. HE then tears the remainder of the front page into small pieces. Behind him TROUGHTON enters from Barbara's hall URC, closing door behind him. JOHN, not realizing Troughton's presence, proceeds to put the torn pieces of the front page into the remainder of the newspaper and screw the lot up into a ball. JOHN moves to DR and picks up the wastebin. HE stuffs the remains of the newspaper into it.*

Unnoticed by John, TROUGHTON, smiling, has moved down to behind John. As JOHN is about to spit his mouthful of paper into the wastebin, TROUGHTON pats him on the back.)

TROUGHTON. (*As HE pats John.*) Mr. Smith!

(*The pat on the back makes JOHN swallow the paper in
his mouth. [N.B. The actor need only mime swallowing
the paper!] JOHN then looks round and does a "double-
take" on seeing Troughton smiling at him. JOHN
chokes and, for want of something better to do, hands
Troughton the wastebin as though it were a prize cup.*
MUSIC: "Love and Marriage* ")

CURTAIN

---

*See cautionary note in front matter.

ACT II

The action is continuous. TROUGHTON is smiling at John. JOHN is looking very sick. TROUGHTON replaces wastebin.

TROUGHTON. You certainly get around in that taxi of yours, Mr. Smith.

(JOHN indicates he can't talk for a moment because of his stomach.)

TROUGHTON. Eaten something that disagreed with you?

(JOHN indicates he won't be a moment and starts to back away towards kitchen DL. TROUGHTON follows.)

TROUGHTON. No hurry. Take your time. When you've pulled yourself together you can explain what you're doing here, can't you?

(JOHN, who is thinking madly, stops DLC. HE then holds his hand up to indicate that he won't be a moment. HE goes over to the kitchen door and gently turns the key in the door. HE then returns to Troughton and walks him to DC.)

JOHN. I think I ought to tell you something.
TROUGHTON. Good.
JOHN. It's about this flat.
TROUGHTON. Yes.

JOHN. It's mine.

(*TROUGHTON stops. So does JOHN.*)

TROUGHTON. Yours?

JOHN. Yes.

TROUGHTON. You didn't say anything about that when I saw you earlier this morning—at your other flat in Wimbledon.

JOHN. Er—no.

TROUGHTON. Even when I mentioned to you that there was a John Smith who resided in a flat in Streatham.

JOHN. Er—no.

TROUGHTON. Slipped your memory, did it?

JOHN. Er—no. There—er—is no *other* John Smith. Only me.

TROUGHTON. I see.

JOHN. Both flats are mine.

TROUGHTON. I see.

JOHN. But er Mary—Mrs. Smith—doesn't know I have this flat.

TROUGHTON. (*Suddenly smiling.*) I see.

JOHN. Yes. It's a little place I keep for—er—er—

TROUGHTON. (*Blandly.*) Collecting stamps?

JOHN. (*After a pause.*) Something like that, yes. My little "den." Where I go for peace and quiet.

TROUGHTON. That's what I reckon too. I reckon you've got some little piece here you want to keep quiet about.

JOHN. No! (*Laughs.*) Nothing like that.

TROUGHTON. I reckon you're leading a double life.

JOHN. (*Laughs more.*) No!

(*The kitchen door handle is turned and loudly rattled by Barbara. JOHN smiles at Troughton and then looks towards kitchen.*)

BARBARA. (*Off yelling.*) Hey! The door's locked!

JOHN. (*To Troughton, smoothly.*) That's my daily help. Yes. Sweet little girl. (*Moves towards the kitchen.*) Get on with your work, Barbara!

BARBARA. (*Off, yells.*) What?

JOHN. (*Calls through door.*) I'll be with you in a minute, Barbara.

BARBARA. (*Off.*) Open the door, you silly fool!

JOHN. (*To Troughton.*) They're so bloody cheeky these days.

BARBARA. (*Off, yells.*) Hey!

(*The door handled is RATTLED furiously.*)

JOHN. (*To Troughton.*) If I don't lock her in she gets nothing done. (*Calls.*) Get on with your work, Barbara! (*Smiles at Troughton and moves nonchalantly back to him at C.*)

TROUGHTON. Very nice—being able to afford a daily.

JOHN. She's more like a weekly. Yes. Couple of hours. Not expensive.

(*Barbara's front DOORBELL goes.*)

JOHN. (*Calls to kitchen.*) I'll go.

TROUGHTON. No. Allow me. I think I'd rather you stayed here, Mr. Smith. Don't want you wandering off again, do we? Banging your head again, do we?

(*During the above speech TROUGHTON moves URC.
TROUGHTON exits into Barbara's hall URC. There is
BANGING from kitchen door.*)

BARBARA. (*Off.*) Hey!
JOHN. Coming, darling.

(*JOHN opens kitchen door and BARBARA comes in with
tray of coffee.*)

BARBARA. What the blazes are you playing at?
JOHN. (*Foolishly.*) I was larking around, darling.
(*Looks nervously towards the hall.*)
BARBARA. (*Walks in front of him.*) I don't know
what's come over you.
JOHN. It's frustration. Come on.
BARBARA. What?
JOHN. (*Takes her towards bedroom.*) I want us both to
go to bed. Now. And have really crazy sex.
BARBARA. I thought we were going out to lunch.
JOHN. To hell with that. I feel right dandy.
BARBARA. (*Tartly.*) It's probably all that newspaper
you've eaten.
JOHN. (*Hurries to bedroom door at R and opens it.*)
Whatever it is I don't want to waste it.
BARBARA. Can't we have our coffee first?

(*SHE goes to sit on settee but JOHN grabs her and propels
her to bedroom door.*)

JOHN. No, we'll save it for after. Go on. Get yourself
stripped, you gorgeous animal.
BARBARA. Hang on. Didn't the doorbell go just now?
JOHN. Yes, yes. You get into bed. I'll see them off.
(*HE pushes her into the bedroom with coffee and closes the*

door, then almost without thinking, HE opens the door and calls in.) Don't start without me.

(*HE closes the door and then locks it as TROUGHTON returns. JOHN quickly leans nonchalantly against the bedroom door, putting the key in his pocket.*)

TROUGHTON. Look who's arrived. It's Mr. Gardner!
STANLEY. (*Hurries in from hall. HE looks very distraught. As he enters:*) I'm ever so sorry, John!
JOHN. (*Aghast.*) Oh, no!

(*JOHN turns and leans his head against the wall DR. STANLEY stands above chair DR. TROUGHTON moves above settee and DLC.*)

TROUGHTON. (*To John.*) I expect he thinks this is the labour exchange, does he?
JOHN. (*Turns and moves to C.*) Oh, well—I suppose the game's up!
STANLEY. (*Moves in to John.*) Oh, Gawd!
JOHN. It's all right, Stanley. I couldn't expect to get away with it for ever.
TROUGHTON. You don't have to say anything, sir.
JOHN. No, I want to.
TROUGHTON. If there's any criminal offense involved, Mr. Smith, you might care to speak to your solicitor.
STANLEY. Bloody hell!
JOHN. Don't worry, Stanley. You'll be all right.
STANLEY. It's *you* I'm worried about.
JOHN. That's noble, Stanley, considering your position.
STANLEY. *My* position?

JOHN. (*To Troughton.*) And we don't need a solicitor. (*To Stanley.*) It's not "illegal" any more, is it, Stanley?

(*STANLEY looks blank. JOHN looks from Stanley to TROUGHTON and then back to Stanley, who is still looking blank, the implication not having dawned.*)

STANLEY. (*Finally.*) What isn't?
JOHN. (*To Stanley.*) Shall I tell him or will you?
TROUGHTON. Tell me what?
JOHN. I thought you'd guessed, Sergeant.
STANLEY. Guessed what?
JOHN. The reason for me having two flats. Stanley and I are like that.

(*STANLEY still looks blank.*)

TROUGHTON. Like what?
JOHN. We're that way inclined.

(*JOHN flicks his head in Stanley's direction. STANLEY puts his hands on his hips in perplexity.*)

TROUGHTON. (*To John.*) What do you mean, sir?
JOHN. Well, you know—

(*JOHN puts his hand on his hip in an effeminate manner. HE then sees that Stanley happens to be standing there in a similar posture and indicates this to Troughton.*
The implication suddenly hits Stanley who is mortified. STANLEY clasps his hand to his mouth and points an accusing finger at John.)

JOHN. Yes, "The love that dare not speak its name."

(*STANLEY backs away to the chair DR.*)

JOHN. (*With sincerity.*) You see, Sergeant, this "dear" man took the flat in Wimbledon above Mrs. Smith and myself and well, it was love at first sight, wasn't it, Stan?

(*STANLEY sits, still with his mouth open.*)

JOHN. He's choked! Well, I fought it—God knows, I fought it. I'd always been normal, you see. Stan is queer from way back.

(*STANLEY, in his frustration, turns around and kneels in the chair.*)

JOHN. But finally—well, I succumbed. Of course I soon realized I couldn't go on deceiving my dear wife in our own home, so Stan and I found this little place. Our little "love-nest."

TROUGHTON. (*At a loss.*) Well, I don't know what to say.

STANLEY. (*Rises, white with anger. Looking round.*) Well, I do! (*Moves to John.*) I'm sorry, John—

JOHN. (*Steps in and stops him.*) No more than I am, darling!

STANLEY. (*Glares at him.*) I've done my best!

JOHN. And I've no complaints, precious!

STANLEY. (*Glares at him.*) I am not *gay!*

JOHN. Well, I'm not too happy about it either!! (*To Troughton.*) I mean, it's a very delicate situation, Sergeant. If my Mary discovered I was—er—you know – AC-DC.

STANLEY. AC-DC?!

JOHN. (*Tapping Stanley's wrist.*) Don't get in a tizzy, Stanley.

BARBARA. (*Off, yells.*) Hey!

*(The bedroom door handle is turned, then RATTLED
followed by a KNOCK. The MEN look at it. There is
further knocking from the other side of the bedroom
door.)*

JOHN. That's Barbara again. Cleaning the bedroom.
I've had to lock her in as usual, Stanley. *Staff* is such a
headache, these days.

BARBARA. *(Off, yells.)* Hey! *(SHE rattles the door
handle.)*

JOHN. *(Marches to bedroom door DR. Calls.)* Stop that
and get on with cleaning the "loo."

BARBARA. *(Off, yells.)* Get lost!

(The MEN react.)

JOHN. *(To Stanley.)* You'll have to speak to her, Stan.
You're the only one she'll listen to. *(Calls.)* I've got *Mr.
Gardner* with me! You know—*(In strong West Country
burr.)* Mr. *Gardener!*

BARBARA. *(Off, yells.)* Mr. Gardener?!

JOHN. *(Calls.)* Yes.

BARBARA. *(Off.)* You mean that funny fellow?

JOHN. *(Quickly.)* That's the one!

*(JOHN points at Stanley. TROUGHTON looks at Stanley
who looks miserable.)*

JOHN. *(Calls.)* You can leave Mr. Gardner and I on our
own Barbara.

BARBARA. *(Off.)* What's he doing here?!

JOHN. *(Calls.)* Don't let it upset you, Barbara.

BARBARA. *(Off.)* Has he brought his cucumber with
him?

(*The three MEN react.*)

JOHN. (*To Troughton.*) Barbara doesn't really approve of Stanley. She's very straight and with him being rather bent—(*HE shrugs sadly, calls.*) Don't bother us for a moment, Barbara.

BARBARA. (*Off.*) I won't!

STANLEY. I would like to say, *categorically*—

JOHN. (*Cutting in.*) And you said it very well, Stanley. (*HE crosses to Troughton.*) He's been practising.

TROUGHTON. (*Warily.*) I think maybe I'll be going, Mr. Smith.

JOHN. Oh, *must* you.

TROUGHTON. Yes. It looks as though I've put two and two together and made it come up five.

JOHN. We all make mistakes. And there won't be any need for this to go further, will there?

TROUGHTON. I suppose not, no.

JOHN. Stan and I would be awfully grateful, wouldn't we, ducky?

(*JOHN puts his arm through Stanley's. STANLEY pulls his arm away, marches DR and sits in chair.*)

TROUGHTON. (*To John.*) And I think you ought to get back home to your wife, Mr. Smith.

JOHN. Mary?

TROUGHTON. You'll probably be needed there to look after her. She's had some very distressing news.

JOHN. Has she?

TROUGHTON. Yes. About her grandparents.

JOHN. (*Blankly.*) Her grandparents?

TROUGHTON. Mr. Gardner, knows all about it. He was there when Mrs. Smith received the sad tidings.

JOHN. What—er—sad tidings exactly?

TROUGHTON. (*To Stanley.*) Shall I tell him or will you, sir?

STANLEY. (*Petulantly.*) I don't care who tells him.

TROUGHTON. That sounds a bit callous.

STANLEY. (*Rises angrily and moves DR.*) I *feel* callous!

TROUGHTON. (*Moves to Stanley.*) Now, look here just because you and Mrs. Smith are rivals for his affections—!

JOHN. (*To Troughton.*) Hang on! What exactly has happened to Mary's grandparents?

TROUGHTON. They fell over the edge of a mountain.

KRIS. (*Takes this in.*) Mountain/

TROUGHTON. Yes, sir. Snowdon.

JOHN. (*Takes this in.*) Snowdon?

TROUGHTON. Yes, sir.

JOHN. I didn't even know they'd come back from Sydney.

TROUGHTON. (*Tries to take this in. Blankly.*) Sydney?

STANLEY. (*Flatly.*) They've been staying with Mary's brother, Sydney.

(*TROUGHTON looks to John. JOHN looks at him blankly. TROUGHTON looks back at Stanley.*)

STANLEY. (*Flatly.*) Sydney lives in Basingstoke.

JOHN. (*Moves, confused, to DC.*) Could we start at the beginning, please.

TROUGHTON. (*Moves to John.*) I'm afraid they're both dead, sir.

JOHN. Mary's grandparents?

TROUGHTON. Yes, sir.

JOHN. *Both* of them?

TROUGHTON. Yes, sir. They were on a hiking holiday apparently. It must come as a bit of a shock.

JOHN. It does. Mary's grandfather's been in a wheel chair for 25 years now.

STANLEY. (*Flatly.*) But apparently his wife would push him *anywhere*.

(*During the ensuing dialogue, MARY enters from kitchen DL. SHE hesitates, looks at her watch and then decides to make a phone call. SHE checks with piece of paper by phone at L of settee and dials. SHE then sits DL waiting for the telephone to be answered.*)

TROUGHTON. Anyway, at a time like this, Mr. Smith, you'll probably want to be with your wife.

JOHN. (*Crosses in front of Troughton to Stanley D.R.*) Yes, of course. It will have knocked her sideways—it certainly has me. I'll get Mr. Gardner to—er—fill me in with a few more "details" and then I'll hurry back to Mary.

TROUGHTON. (*Pointedly.*) Yes and if I were you, sir, I'd *stay* with Mary.

(*Barbara's telephone RINGS. JOHN is not sure whether to answer it. HE looks at Stanley. STANLEY turns away unhelpfully. After a moment, TROUGHTON, who is beside the telephone, picks it up.*)

TROUGHTON. (*On phone.*) Hello!

MARY. (*On phone.*) Is that 674-3105?

TROUGHTON. (*Quickly checks with dial–on phone.*) Yes. Detective Sergeant Troughton speaking.

MARY. (*On phone.*) Oh, good. I got straight through this time. (*TROUGHTON frowns.*) It's Mrs. Smith speaking.

TROUGHTON. (*On phone, surprised.*) Mrs. Smith?

(*JOHN and STANLEY react. JOHN grabs hold of Stanley.*)

MARY.(*On phone.*) From Kenilworth Avenue. You called on us earlier this morning.

TROUGHTON. (*On phone, confused.*) Yes, I remember. (*To John.*) I thought your wife didn't know anything about this place?

JOHN. (*Horrified.*) She doesn't.

STANLEY. (*Moves to Troughton.*) I think I can ex–

TROUGHTON. (*Cutting.*) You shut up!

MARY. (*On phone.*) Hello?

TROUGHTON. (*On phone.*) Sorry, Mrs. Smith. Somebody was interrupting.

MARY. (*On phone.*) Trouble on the line again?

TROUGHTON. (*On phone.*) Beg pardon?

MARY. (*On phone.*) The last time I dialled this number all I got was heavy breathing.

TROUGHTON. (*On phone.*) Heavy breathing. I see! (*HE looks at John and Stanley.*)

STANLEY. I think she's got hold of the wrong—

TROUGHTON. (*To Stanley.*) Shut up and sit down.

(*HE pulls Stanley across him and STANLEY sits L corner of settee.*)

MARY. (*On phone.*) Well, I'm very worried about my husband's behavior.

TROUGHTON. (*On phone.*) Mr. Smith's behavior?

JOHN. What's she saying?

TROUGHTON. You shut up as well, Tinkerbell!

(*HE pulls John across and JOHN sits beside Stanley on settee.*)

MARY. (*On phone.*) Yes, he's been acting very very queer just lately.

TROUGHTON. (*On phone.*) Queer, I see.

(*JOHN and STANLEY exchange a glance.*)

TROUGHTON. (*To John.*) I think she may have sussed you out.

MARY. (*On phone.*) He rang me to say he'd be home in less than five minutes and that was twenty minutes ago. So, you know, I'm getting anxious with everything else that's happened.

TROUGHTON. (*On phone.*) Yes. I still don't quite understand why you're ringing *this* number.

STANLEY. I think I can ex— (*Starts to rise.*)

TROUGHTON. Sit!

(*STANLEY sits.*)

MARY. (*On phone, beginning to get exasperated.*) I'm ringing because of my husband.

TROUGHTON. (*On phone, surprised.*) Because of your—(*To John and Stanley.*) Oh, yes, your cover's been blown my darlings.

(*JOHN and STANLEY look worried.*)

MARY. (*On phone.*) Hello?

TROUGHTON. (*On phone.*) Sorry, Mrs. Smith. I was just trying to ascertain why you would ring this particular number.

MARY. (*On phone, becoming irritated.*) Because it's yours!

TROUGHTON. (*On phone, mystified.*) Mine?

MARY. (*On phone.*) Isn't this a good place to get you?

TROUGHTON. (*On phone, affronted.*) What, *me*, *here*??!

(*STANLEY and JOHN look perplexed at Troughton's agitation.*)

MARY. (*On phone.*) Yes. You and the men.

TROUGHTON. (*On phone, more affronted.*) What men?

(*STANLEY and JOHN exchange another worried glance as THEY try to work out what Mary could be saying on the other end of the line.*)

MARY. (*On phone.*) The men you have under you.

TROUGHTON. (*On phone.*) Eh?!!

(*JOHN and STANLEY exchange a look.*)

MARY. (*On phone.*) Don't you all operate from there?

TROUGHTON. (*Breaks angrily DR. On phone.*) Now wait a minute, Mrs. Smith. Don't try and implicate *me* in your husband's activities.

(*JOHN and STANLEY rise, worried. MARY breaks angrily DL.*)

MARY. (*On phone.*) I thought that's what you were paid to do!

TROUGHTON. (*On phone.*) Well, I'm not!

MARY. (*On phone, getting upset.*) I suppose it's too little a thing for you to handle!

TROUGHTON. (*On phone, disgusted.*) That's lovely, that is! (*To John.*) I'm not listening to this any more!

JOHN/STANLEY. (*Together.*) (*Anxiously.*) Just ring off, please/If you'd let me explain.

TROUGHTON. Shut up!

MARY. (*On phone.*) Hello!

TROUGHTON. (*On phone, pressing on.*) I'm sorry Mrs. Smith, but there's far too much smearing of the police going on these days. I'm an absolutely straight and normal officer I am, and it's not my fault if your husband and Mr. Gardner are a couple of pansies!

(*JOHN and STANLEY sit once again in horror.*)

MARY. (*On phone, shocked.*) Pansies?

TROUGHTON. (*On phone.*) I'm sad to say your suspicions are correct. Mr. Gardner's one from way back and your husband's just turned.

(*JOHN and STANLEY bury their heads.*)

MARY. (*On phone.*) Just turned?

TROUGHTON. (*On phone.*) Yes.

MARY. (*On phone.*) But John smokes a pipe.

TROUGHTON. (*On phone.*) I don't care if he smokes kippers, he's a nancy.

(*JOHN and STANLEY look up.*)

MARY. (*On phone.*) Oh my God! (*Sits, mortified, in chair DL.*)

TROUGHTON. (*On phone.*) I'm with them both now. They've admitted to it.

MARY. (*On phone, in disbelief.*) John and Stanley?

TROUGHTON. (*On phone.*) I'm sorry if it's been a shock to you but you were already on to them, weren't you?

MARY. (*On phone.*) And you're with them now?

TROUGHTON. (*On phone.*) In my *official* capacity, Mrs. Smith and that is all.

MARY. (*On phone.*) You haven't arrested them, though, have you?

TROUGHTON. (*On phone.*) No. It's not illegal now, is it?

MARY. (*On phone.*) Then why are they at the Police Station?

TROUGHTON. (*On phone.*) No, no. they're at their flat in Streatham—47 Lewin Road, Streatham, S.W. 16.

(*Mortified, JOHN and STANLEY stand up, turn around and slowly start to tip-toe ULC. At the other end of the telephone Mary's mind is racing.*)

TROUGHTON. (*On phone.*) Hello?! Hello?!

(*MARY puts the phone down and walks quickly out into her hall ULC.*)

TROUGHTON. (*On phone.*) Mrs. Smith! (*HE turns to where John and Stanley were sitting.*) You wife seems— (*He sees they are tiptoeing behind settee to Barbara's hall door URC. Calls.*) Oi!

(*JOHN and STANLEY stop and clutch each other. TROUGHTON walks up R.*)

TROUGHTON. And where do you think you're off to, girls?

JOHN. I think I ought to get home and comfort my wife.

STANLEY. And I'll try to find someone to comfort *me*.

TROUGHTON. (*To Stanley.*) I reckon the best place *you* can go is abroad.

STANLEY. That's not a bad idea.

TROUGHTON. Well, I'll get back to the station and make my report. (*Opens hall door, URC.*)

STANLEY. (*To John.*) I think we should tell him that someone's got hold of the wrong end of the stick.

TROUGHTON. That's one way of putting it! It seems to me that Mr. Smith had a perfectly happy and normal marriage until you came mincing into his life. (*Realizes HE has inadvertently placed his hand on his hips. HE quickly removes them and exits URC.*)

STANLEY. (*To John.*) You rotten devil!

JOHN. (*Marches DLC.*) Oh, shut up What about *me*? He just told my wife I'm a pansy.

STANLEY. (*Marches DRC and meets John DC.*) He told her *I* was one, too! He thinks I'm a practicing homosexual!

JOHN. Well, if you're only *practicing!* (*Moves furiously UL.*)

STANLEY. (*Moves R and sits in chair.*) He's going to put it in a report. It'll be on police records that I'm a poof.

JOHN. Oh, belt up a minute.

STANLEY. I'll probably be inundated.

JOHN. Stop thinking about yourself. He gave Mary this address. I'll ring her and say I'm on my way home to explain. (*Moves above settee to Barbara's phone at R end of settee and dials Mary's number.*)

STANLEY. Homosexual! God, I have trouble convincing some people I'm homo sapiens.

JOHN. If you'd stayed in Wimbledon none of this would have happened.

STANLEY. You are ungrateful! I came to tell you that your picture's in the papers.

JOHN. I know!

STANLEY. I had to tear it up!

JOHN. I had to bloody well eat it up!

(*The PHONE rings in Mary's flat.*)

STANLEY. Why the dickens don't you simply confess?

JOHN. I was doing all right till you started helping me! There's no reply! She's probably fainted.

(*The bedroom door is RATTLED.*)

BARBARA. (*Off.*) Hey! John!

STANLEY. Your staff's getting difficult now.

JOHN. (*Puts phone down and unlocks the door DR. Calls, as he does so.*) Coming, darling!

BARBARA. (*Enters from bedroom*) What's going on in here? Oh!

JOHN. You haven't met my farming friend, Mr. Gardner, have you?

BARBARA. (*Coldly.*) No.

JOHN. Mr. Gardner was just leaving. Wasn't it sweet of Stanley to drive over?

BARBARA. (*Coldly.*) Yes.

JOHN. We've had lovely chats. Do you know, his Jersey cow has still not discovered a mate.

BARBARA. (*Coldly.*) Really.

JOHN. Yes. (*Moving to Stanley.*) Why do you reckon that is, Mr. Gardner?

STANLEY. (*Flatly.*) Maybe all the Staffordshire bulls are gay.

JOHN. (*Considers this.*) Mm. Yes. Poofy bulls could be. Well, I'm sorry I can't advise you. It's not really my line of country.

(*BARBARA moves in.*)

BARBARA. (*To Stanley.*) And he'd be very grateful if you'd stop involving him. We're not interested in farming!

STANLEY. Who the hell is?!

JOHN. It's all right, Stanley. My wife doesn't mean to be rude.

BARBARA. (*To John.*) Yes, I do. This is supposed to be our day off together and you seem more keen to spend it discussing bloody cattle with Stanley. (*Decisively.*) Right! I'm going to get ready for bed. (*To John.*) You can either join me or go back to Stanley's farm and bed down with him. (*Moves angrily DR towards bedroom as the front DOORBELL goes. SHE stops. To Stanley.*) That's probably one of his old cows now. (*Storms out into the hall URC.*)

JOHN. (*To Stanley.*) *Now* look what you've done.

STANLEY. Me?

JOHN. Yes. You've ruined *both* my marriages.

STANLEY. (*As HE sits petulantly in chair DR.*) The only person who's ruined round here is me.

(*A flustered BOBBY enters from the hall followed by Barbara. BOBBY is carrying a paint roller which is covered in red paint.*)

BOBBY. (*As HE enters.*) Have you looked at your ceiling? (*Moves DR followed by Barbara.*)

BARBARA. (*To Bobby.*) I can't say I've noticed anything coming through.

(*BARBARA and BOBBY are both looking up at the ceiling.*)

BOBBY. The whole bloody lot went over! Two gallons of red paint, my dear. Ver-bloody-million! (*To John.*) Sorry to intrude, ducky, I told you I'd get familiar. Finished your newspaper, did you?

JOHN. Yes!

BOBBY. (*Chuckling.*) What did you have for dessert? Readers Digest.

(*JOHN moves angrily upstage and Bobby notices Stanley sitting there in the chair DR.*)

BARBARA. (*Cheerfully.*) Hello!

(*STANLEY reacts to Bobby's "gay" character and slowly crosses his legs.*)

STANLEY. (*Finally, in deep manly voice.*) Hello!

BARBARA. Mr. Gardner's a farming friend of my husband's.

BOBBY. Oh, yes! King Edward, pleased to meet you, your Highness.

JOHN. Thank you!

BOBBY. (*Seriously, to John.*) No, it's no joke my darling, red paint all over the bathroom floor. I'm worried it may be coming through your ceiling.

JOHN. (*Impatiently.*) I'm sure it isn't.

BOBBY. (*Pressing on.*) You see, I'm thinking that our bathroom is probably over yours. (*Wandering around the room trying to work out where his bathroom above might be.*)

JOHN. (*Following Bobby.*) I wouldn't know. It doesn't matter.

BOBBY. I'll go and bang on our bathroom floor and you listen. Your bathroom is probably directly beneath.

JOHN. (*Tries to escort Bobby URC towards hall door.*) It's *all right.*

BOBBY. You don't want it seeping through, dear—
especially if you're sitting in the bath.

(*BOBBY moves towards hall door URC. Barbara's front
DOORBELL goes. BOBBY turns in doorway.*)

BOBBY. BOBBY will get it!

(*BOBBY exits into hall URC. JOHN breaks R. STANLEY
rises and takes a pace ULC.*)

STANLEY. Well, I think I may as well be shoving off
now.
BARBARA. (*Moves UR behind settee. Sarcastically.*)
Oh, must you?
JOHN. Good idea. You might care to give me a ring
later. (*Pointedly.*) Let me know how things are at the farm.
BARBARA. Yes, do keep up the bulletins.
PORTERHOUSE. (*Cheerfully enters from hall URC.*)
Gentleman on the way out said "Go right in."

(*Unnoticed by the others, STANLEY ducks behind chair
DL.*)

PORTERHOUSE. (*To John.*) Sergeant Porterhouse
again, sir.
JOHN. (*Jovially.*) Yes. Porterhouse from Streatham.
PORTERHOUSE. (*To John.*) Sorry to barge in once
more.
JOHN. (*Jovially.*) That's O.K.
BARBARA. Yes, the more the merrier. If you want
anything from, me, Sergeant, I shall be in bed. (*SHE exits
into bedroom.*)
PORTERHOUSE. (*Follows her DR.*) I don't think
that'll be necessary—

(*BARBARA has gone and closed the door. STANLEY puts the wastebin, DL on his head and starts to crawl towards the kitchen DL.*)

PORTERHOUSE. (*To John.*) Seems a bit upset.

JOHN. (*Joins Porterhouse DR.*) Nothing serious. What can I do for you, Sergeant?

PORTERHOUSE. I just thought you'd like to know that I— (*Suddenly notices Stanley.*) Oh.

(*JOHN looks and reacts to Stanley [still with wastebin on head] who is on his hands and knees by kitchen door with his hand on the door handle. STANLEY gently opens kitchen door while JOHN crosses to him.*)

JOHN. Hey!

(*As JOHN speaks HE hits the top of the wastebin. STANLEY closes kitchen door with a bang but stays on his hands and knees with his back to them.*)

JOHN. We have a visitor.

STANLEY. (*Hesitates and then turns round but remains on his knees. HE removes the wastebin from his head.*) We've met.

PORTERHOUSE. (*Moves in to below settee at D.C. Surprised.*) Mr. Smith!

JOHN. (*Turning.*) Yes?

PORTERHOUSE. (*To John, chuckling.*) No, no. The *other* Mr. Smith.

JOHN. Other Mr. Smith?

STANLEY. Your namesake. From Wimbledon.

JOHN. (*Slowly turns to look at Stanley then smiles hugely.*) Yes! (*To Porterhouse.*) Mr. Smith dropped in to introduce himself.

STANLEY. Yes. I dropped in—landed here.

PORTERHOUSE. (*Chuckling, to John.*) I bet you were surprised when he turned up.

JOHN. I was actually, yes.

PORTERHOUSE. (*Enjoying it.*) Two John Smiths, taxi drivers, abrasion of the cranium. It's a million to one chance.

STANLEY. It's almost unbelievable.

PORTERHOUSE. Yes! (*To John.*) Anyway, it's all O.K. (*Indicates Stanley.*) Mr. Smith here verified the situation vis-a-vis the mix up over the names at the hospital.

(*JOHN shakes Stanley's hand and pulls him off his knees.*)

JOHN. (*To Stanley.*) Thanks, John.

STANLEY. Don't mention it, John.

PORTERHOUSE. So, no problems!

JOHN. No problems! Thanks for calling. (*Moves in front of Porterhouse to indicate that Porterhouse may leave.*)

PORTERHOUSE. (*To Stanley.*) And I'm sorry if I arrived at that slightly inopportune moment this morning, Mr. Smith.

STANLEY. (*Laughing it off.*) Oh.

PORTERHOUSE. (*To John.*) He was planning to get Mrs. Smith into bed.

JOHN. (*Takes this in. Flatly.*) Was he?

STANLEY. (*Crosses in front of Porterhouse, to John, pointedly.*) I'm sure you can understand it was a very delicate situation.

PORTERHOUSE. (*To Stanley.*) We're used to getting involved with domestic squabbles. But like I said to Mrs. Smith after you'd gone, don't take it out on Stanley.

JOHN. (*Thinks for a moment.*) Hang on a second—

STANLEY. Stanley is my little boy.

JOHN. Ah.

STANLEY. Mary's and mine.

JOHN. Ah.

STANLEY. *Little* Stanley! (*HE indicates the height of a young boy.*)

JOHN. *Little* Stanley, yes! (*He indicates the height, too.*)

(*BARBARA enters from the bedroom DR. She is wearing her flowing negligee once more. SHE ignores everyone but John.*)

BARBARA. (*To John.*) I've decided to give you five minutes to join me in bed.

JOHN. (*Hurries to her at bedroom door.*) Darling, we've got *visitors.*

PORTERHOUSE. (*Crosses in front of Stanley.*) Don't mind me, I'm broadminded. (*To Stanley.*) It must be catching. Wednesday morning—NWW.

(*PORTERHOUSE chuckles. BARBARA crosses in front of John to Porterhouse.*)

BARBARA. (*Over polite.*) Are you staying long, Sergeant?

PORTERHOUSE. I'm just on my way, Mrs. Smith. (*Refers to Stanley.*) I bet *you* got a surprise, too, when this gentleman turned up.

BARBARA. Nothing he does would surprise me.

PORTERHOUSE. (*Chuckling.*) With them having so much in common though.

BARBARA. Don't tell me, bullocks!

PORTERHOUSE. Beg pardon?

JOHN. (*Pulls her back to bedroom door. Hastily.*) I'll be with you in a jiffy, darling. Less than five minutes.

BARBARA. And in that time perhaps you could resolve your future relationship with Stanley.

(*The above remark leaves Porterhouse confused as BARBARA exits into bedroom. JOHN looks round to Porterhouse.*)

PORTERHOUSE. (*To Stanley.*) His relationship with Stanley?

STANLEY. (*Confused.*) It's quite easy to explain.

JOHN. (*Quickly, to Porterhouse.*) Mrs. Smith and I were suggesting to the other Mr. Smith (*HE indicates Stanley.*) that he may care to have "Little Stanley" fostered with us here.

(*PORTERHOUSE looks at Stanley. STANLEY closes his eyes in anguish, moves to the chair DL and sits.*)

PORTERHOUSE. (*To John.*) Fostered?

JOHN. (*Hoarsely.*) Just a suggestion.

PORTERHOUSE. (*To Stanley.*) Are things as bad as that at home?

STANLEY. And getting worse!

PORTERHOUSE. (*To John.*) It might be the best thing for the little lad.

JOHN. (*To Porterhouse.*) Yes, I'll see you out.

PORTERHOUSE. (*Moving.*) Right.

(*Barbara's front DOORBELL goes. JOHN stops
    Porterhouse from moving.*)

JOHN. On second thoughts—I'm sure you'd like a cup
of tea, Sergeant. (*Moves Porterhouse to L. end of settee.*)
    PORTERHOUSE. Tea?
    JOHN. (*Moves to door URC as HE speaks the
following:*) Mr. Smith, why don't you take the Sergeant
into the kitchen and put the kettle on while I open the front
door and (*Becoming slightly hysterical.*) deal with whoever
it may be. (*Exits into hall URC.*)
    PORTERHOUSE. (*To Stanley.*) Cup of tea would go
down very nice, actually sir.
    STANLEY. (*Opens kitchen door.*) After you, Sergeant.
    PORTERHOUSE. (*Moves into doorway.*) Rightio. (*To
Stanley.*) We'll have a good old chat over a cuppa. You tell
me all about your problems with little Stanley. (*Exits into
kitchen DL.*)
    STANLEY. (*Thinking of John–to himself.*) "Little
Stanley" is likely to get arrested for bloody murder!

(*STANLEY exits into kitchen DL. JOHN returns from the
    hall URC in a state of shock. HE thinks for a moment
    and then hurries to the kitchen door and opens it.*)

JOHN. (*Calling urgently.*) Stanley!
    STANLEY. (*Appears in kitchen doorway. Growling.*)
Stanley's at bloody school!

(*STANLEY disappears. JOHN's face remains blank   HE
    considers this.*)

JOHN. (*Calling, lightly.*) Stanley's father. Mr. Smith!
    STANLEY. (*Appears. Curtly.*) What is it?

JOHN. (*Sweetly.*) May I have a little word, Mr. Smith. (*HE pulls Stanley across him, calls sweetly into kitchen.*) Won't keep Mr. Smith a second, Sergeant.) Help yourself to "biccies." (*JOHN closes the door and rushes to Stanley DC below settee.*) Disaster!

STANLEY. What?

JOHN. Mary.

STANLEY. Mary? What about her?

JOHN. Outside.

STANLEY. No!

JOHN. I went to answer the bell. Opened the front door—Mary.

STANLEY. What did you do?

JOHN. I nearly died.

STANLEY. What did she *do?*

JOHN. She didn't have the time to do anything. I slammed the door in her face.

(*Barbara's front DOORBELL goes.*)

STANLEY. I don't think she took the hint.

JOHN. (*Moves in front of Stanley, looking towards hall door URC.*) No.

STANLEY. Did she look cross?

JOHN. She looked like a woman who'd just been told her husband was a pansy.

STANLEY. Yes. I can imagine that look.

JOHN. (*Pulls Stanley across him to DRC.*) You go and deal with her, Stanley.

STANLEY. (*Stopping.*) Me?! She thinks I'm the one who turned you.

JOHN. Well, anything's better than her finding out about Barbara.

(*Barbara's front DOORBELL rings more urgently. JOHN moves to DLC.*)

JOHN. (*Moving.*) Maybe I can get out the back way.
STANLEY. No! (*Moves to John and grabs him.*) That's no good.
JOHN. (*Pulls away.*) It's the best I can think of.
STANLEY. (*Grabs him.*) She's already seen you.
JOHN. (*Attempts to move.*) You deal with it.
STANLEY. (*Grabbing him.*) Don't say "deal with it!"

(*BARBARA still in her negligee enters from bedroom DR and stops on seeing the struggle between John and Stanley. After a moment THEY notice Barbara and smoothly pass their struggle off as a "soft shoe shuffle."*)

BARBARA. Could I interrupt the Floral Dance for a moment?
JOHN. (*Crosses in front of Stanley to Barbara DRC.*) Of course, sweetie. Stanley was just showing me how his potato grading machine works. Fascinating. (*Mimes a mechanical piece of some kind.*)
BARBARA. I don't know if either you or Mr. Gardner have noticed but there is someone at the front door.
JOHN. Yes. I've dealt with it.

(*JOHN puts a comforting arm around Barbara. The front DOORBELL goes again.*)

BARBARA. They don't seem to be aware of that.
JOHN. I've been out to them twice. (*To Stanley.*) Damn nuisance, aren't they?
STANLEY. (*Faintly.*) Yes.
BARBARA. Who is it?

JOHN. You might well ask.

BARBARA. I *am* asking.

JOHN. Yes. It's a nun.

(*JOHN looks at Stanley. STANLEY has to go and sit in his chair DL for comfort.*)

BARBARA. A nun?

JOHN. Yes. From that convent on the other side of Streatham Common.

BARBARA. What does she want?

JOHN. Collecting for charity.

(*The front DOORBELL rings again persistently.*)

JOHN. (*To Stanley.*) I've got an idea.

STANLEY. (*Rising.*) I've got a better one. I'll do the tea, you do the nun! (*Hurries into kitchen DL.*)

BARBARA. (*To John.*) Maybe the nun would like to join you for a cup of tea.

JOHN. I'll sort her out.

BARBARA. You haven't had much luck so far. (*Moving URC.*) I'll go.

JOHN. (*Hurries to her and quickly grabs her. During the following speech HE takes her DR.*) No! If she sees you she'll hit the roof. I'll tell her, two donations is all she's going to get. (*Opens bedroom door DR.*)

BARBARA. Then perhaps you'll be as firm with Mr. Gardner.

JOHN. Oh, yes.

BARBARA. Because if you don't come to bed, my lad, *right now,* I'll go and stay in a hotel—by myself. (*Flaunts into the bedroom.*)

JOHN. (*Calls.*) If you do, could you go out the back way?!

(*JOHN locks bedroom door and hurries into hall URC. The kitchen door DL opens and STANLEY backs in followed by Mary. THEY end up at DC.*)

STANLEY. Just hold your horses, Mary!

MARY. I've been at that front door for ages.

STANLEY. Well, you found the back way in.

MARY. Now what's going on here and what are you and John doing in Streatham and what's all this about you being a couple of pansies?

STANLEY. One question at a time please.

PORTERHOUSE. (*Nervously looks in from the kitchen DL. He now has his jacket off.*) You all right, Mrs. Smith?

MARY. (*Moves to Porterhouse.*) No, I'm not. I want to know what my husband's doing in this flat.

PORTERHOUSE. (*Moves in front of Mary to Stanley at C.*) I'm sure he'll be only too pleased to tell you.

STANLEY. Yes of course he will.

MARY. (*Moves to Porterhouse.*) John slammed the door in my face.

PORTERHOUSE. (*To Stanley.*) Did you?

MARY. (*Shouting at Porterhouse.*) *John* did!

PORTERHOUSE. (*Shouts back.*) I *heard* you!

STANLEY. (*Hurries DL to kitchen door.*) I think we're ready for that tea now, Sergeant.

PORTERHOUSE. All right. (*To Mary.*) But you listen to me, Mrs. Smith. I think what's being proposed here could solve all your problems.

MARY. And what exactly *is* being proposed?

PORTERHOUSE. That Stanley comes to live here with Mr. Smith.

(*MARY looks outraged.*)

STANLEY. (*To Porterhouse.*) Just make the tea! (*Pushes Porterhouse into the kitchen DL and then lays back against the door.*)

MARY. (*To Stanley, furious.*)   You crafty scheming little fairy.

(*SHE advances on Stanley who is behind the settee and who retreats UC followed by Mary.*)

STANLEY. Now, Mary. (*Backs away URC.*)
MARY. There's me thinking John's out driving his taxi every night and all the time he's shacking up with you in Streatham.
JOHN. (*Enters from hall URC not seeing Mary.*) It's all right, she's gone! (*See Mary—yells.*) Ahhhh—hullo, darling! (*Crosses in front of Stanley to Mary ULC. HE gives her a huge hug.*)
MARY. (*Coldly.*) Go on, it's Stanley's turn now.
STANLEY. She's a bit upset.
JOHN. (*Consoling her.*) Oh, dear. Tell me about it on the way home. (*HE pushes her to hall door URC.*)
MARY. You *are* bloody home, aren't you?

(*Marches DRC and in front of settee. JOHN comes DRC. STANLEY comes DLC.*)

JOHN. Not so loud, darling.

(*The bedroom door DR is RATTLED and then there is the sound of BANGING.*
THEY all look in that direction.)

BARBARA. (*Off.*) Hey!

MARY. Who's that?

JOHN. A sort of person, that's all. (*Moves to door DR and calls.*) Won't be a moment. I'm just dealing with the lady who was at the front door.

BARBARA. (*Off.*) I don't care what you're doing. Open this door, *now!*

JOHN. (*Removes key and puts it in his pocket. Calls.*) I think I've lost the key.

BARBARA. (*Off – yells.*) No you haven't—you've locked me in again.

JOHN. (*Calls, to Mary – brightly.*) Off we go, darling.

BARBARA. (*Off.*) Open this door!

MARY. What on earth's going on?

(*There are three loud BANGS on the bedroom door.*)

JOHN. (*To Mary.*) Nothing's going on.

(*Suddenly there is a splintering CRASH and the bedroom door bursts open. BARBARA hurtles into the room and lands on the floor. She is dressed to go out.*

The suitcase with which she has struck the door, flies across the room SHE pulls herself together, whilst JOHN and STANLEY assist her to her feet. MARY moves DR looking bewildered.

PORTERHOUSE pops his head round the kitchen door. HE now carries a kettle.)

PORTERHOUSE. Anyone not take sugar? (*HE takes in the situation.*) I'll let you put your own in.

(*PORTERHOUSE retreats into the kitchen. BARBARA snatches her case from Stanley who has retrieved it.*)

BARBARA. (*To John.*) I shall probably ring you from a hotel. (*To Stanley.*) You can now stay the night if you like. (*To Mary.*) I hope you collect more than I have. (*Moves, then stops and comes back to Mary.*) Don't you normally have a habit?

MARY. (*After a moment's pause.*) Oh, sorry. How do you do?

(*MARY then shakes Barbara's hand thinking that his is the "habit" to which Barbara is referring. BARBARA looks blank for a moment, looks at the two men, then storms out URC into the hall with her suitcase. MARY steps into John below R. end of settee.*)

MARY. What was that all about?

(*There is a pause.*)

JOHN. That was Lofty.
MARY. Lofty?
JOHN. Lofty. Yes. (*Matter-of-fact.*) He's a transvestite.

(*JOHN looks at Stanley. STANLEY walks away and sits in his chair DL with his head in his hands.*)

MARY. (*Amazed.*) A transvestite?
JOHN. A fellow who dresses up on women's clothes.
MARY. I know what a transvestite is!
JOHN. Good.
MARY. (*In disbelief.*) *That* was a *Man?*
JOHN. Yes, Lofty's really amazing when he dolls himself up.
MARY. (*Astonished.*) Is he going to walk down the street like that?
JOHN. Yes.

MARY. It's incredible!

JOHN. (*Nods.*) Yes. (*Deadpan.*) Lofty's a friend of Stanley's. (*Looks towards Stanley who slowly looks up.*)

STANLEY. Lofty is *not* a friend of Stanley's.

JOHN. They've just has a bust-up.

STANLEY. (*Rise. To Mary.*) "Lofty" is a friend of your husband's.

MARY. (*Shocked.*) John!

JOHN. (*Hurries over to Stanley.*) Let's say we share him, Stanley.

MARY. What?!

STANLEY. We *don't* share him!

JOHN. Well, let's not fight over him, Stanley. Poor Mary's had enough shocks for one day haven't you darling?

MARY. I damn well have. You've never shown any of these kinky signs at home.

JOHN. (*Weakly.*) I haven't had the time.

MARY. (*To Stanley.*) I don't think I'm so surprised about you.

(*BOBBY enters from Barbara's hall URC. HE looks furious.*)

BOBBY. (*As he enters.*) Are you all deaf or what?!

(*JOHN and STANLEY break away in despair. JOHN to DR. STANLEY to DL.*)

JOHN. Some other time!

BOBBY. What about my banging?

JOHN. What banging?!

BOBBY. Cyril and I have been banging away up there for ages. Tapping away like Fred Astaire and Ginger Rogers.

JOHN. Never mind!!

BOBBY. (*Points to ceiling.*) But it must be seeping through ducky. (*Sees Mary for the first time. Cheerfully waving.*) Hello!

(*MARY reacts. BOBBY moves to her at DC.*)

BOBBY. You're new around here, aren't you?
MARY. (*Coolly.*) Yes.
BOBBY. I'm from upstairs.
MARY. (*Coldly.*) How do you do.
BOBBY. Nicely thanks. That's a very pretty dress, if I may say so.
MARY. (*Pointedly.*) Yes, it's *mine*.

(*BOBBY looks surprised.*)

JOHN. (*To Bobby.*) Come back later.
BOBBY. Later may be too late, sunshine. There's two gallons of red paint slurping about up there.
JOHN. It'll be all right.
BOBBY. Not the way Cyril's going at it, it won't. Trying to soak it up with that silly little make-up sponge of his. I think our bathroom must be over yours. (*Indicates bedroom*) Yours is through there, is it?

(*BOBBY crosses to bedroom door DR. JOHN grabs his arm.*)

JOHN. I'm sure it won't come through!

(*PORTERHOUSE enters DL from kitchen with tea things on a tray. He is now wearing one of Mary's aprons.*)

PORTERHOUSE. (*Cheerfully.*) Right! Tea's up!

(*THEY all stop and look at him.*)

PORTERHOUSE. Now—who's going to be "mother?"
MARY. (*Looks at Stanley, John and Bobby.*) Take your pick.
PORTERHOUSE.   (*Moves to Mary.*) I'm not superstitious, I'll pour.
MARY. And what exactly are *you* doing here?
PORTERHOUSE. Don't worry, it's not official any more. I'm just being the good fairy.

(*MARY looks at John, who realizes HE still has hold of Bobby's arm. STANLEY slowly closes door DL and moves to Porterhouse.*)

STANLEY. I'd re-phrase that if I were you.
BOBBY. If you'll excuse me, I won't stay for tea. (*To John.*) I must go to your bathroom. I've got to satisfy myself. (*Exits in bedroom DR.*)
JOHN. He's not with us.
PORTERHOUSE. Who's for tea then? (*Moves to back of settee and places tray on table behind settee.*)
JOHN. (*Jovially.*) What a good idea, nice cup of tea!
STANLEY. (*Jovially.*) Oo, cup of tea!
MARY. (*Marches away angrily to URC. Curtly.*) No tea for me, thank you.

(*JOHN and STANLEY sit on the settee. JOHN at R end and STANLEY at L.*)

PORTERHOUSE. Oh. And what about Mrs. Smith?

(*JOHN and STANLEY exchange a glance.*)

MARY. I said "no tea for me."

PORTERHOUSE. (*Chuckles.*) No, I meant the *other* Mrs. Smith.

(*STANLEY and JOHN react to each other.*)

MARY. What *other* Mrs. Smith?
PORTERHOUSE. The one who lives here.

(*MARY moves down to John at R end of settee.*)

JOHN. (*Quickly.*) He means "Lofty."

(*During the ensuing scene PORTERHOUSE pours a cup of tea for Stanley, John and himself. [N.B. The actor playing Porterhouse will find he has plenty of time!]*)

MARY. Oh, that's *very* nice, "Mrs. Smith!"
PORTERHOUSE. (*Chuckling.*) "Lofty!"

(*JOHN and STANLEY look at him.*)

PORTERHOUSE. (*Still chuckling.*) I like it!
MARY. (*To John.*) Has he met Lofty?
JOHN. (*With false gaiety.*) Yes!
MARY. All dolled up?!
JOHN. Yes!
PORTERHOUSE. (*Chuckling.*) "Lofty!"

(*JOHN and STANLEY look at him again. PORTERHOUSE gives Stanley his tea. STANLEY goes to drink.*)

PORTERHOUSE. Do you know what *I* call *mine?*

(*MARY looks astonished as SHE takes in what she thinks
is the implication. JOHN and STANLEY react to each
other because they realize what Mary must be thinking.
JOHN buries his head in his hands as STANLEY bangs
his cup down in the saucer.*)

MARY. (*Finally.*) Yours?!
PORTERHOUSE. (*To Mary.*) Mind you, we've been
together longer than Mr. Smith (*HE indicates John.*) and
his "Lofty."

(*PORTERHOUSE chuckles at Mary who looks blank.
JOHN and STANLEY react to each other.
PORTERHOUSE offers Stanley the sugar.*)

PORTERHOUSE. (*To Mary.*) We've had twenty years
of it.
STANLEY. (*Politely.*) No sugar for me, thank you.
PORTERHOUSE. (*Laughing.*) I call mine "Gruesome."

(*JOHN looks up to heaven. PORTERHOUSE pours
John's tea.*)

PORTERHOUSE. It's just a joke of course.
MARY. God, is everybody at it? (*Sits in chair DR.*)
PORTERHOUSE. It's only a silly sort of game really.
MARY. A game?
JOHN. (*Laughs, foolishly.*) Yes, a game! No harm!
(*Changing the subject; to Porterhouse.*) Two lumps for
me, please!
PORTERHOUSE. (*To Mary.*) Actually, I think my
wife has grown quite accustomed to "Gruesome."

(STANLEY chokes on his tea and JOHN comes to his assistance. MARY is staggered. PORTERHOUSE, oblivious, puts the sugar in John's tea and hands it to him.)

MARY. *(Rising.)* Your wife doesn't mind?

PORTERHOUSE. 'Course not. *She's* got a name for *me*.

MARY. I bet she has.

PORTERHOUSE. Guess what it is.

STANLEY. *(Helpfully.)* Cynthia?

PORTERHOUSE. *(Laughing.)* No, no! *(Moves DRC laughing, carrying his cup of tea.)* Pussy!

(PORTERHOUSE collapses in the chair DL laughing. MARY sits in chair DR fuming. JOHN feigns hysterical laughter for Mary's benefit. STANLEY looks bemused.)

STANLEY. *(Finally.)* Why Pussy?

PORTERHOUSE. *(Chuckling.)* She reckons I'm always purring.

MARY. With such an understanding wife, I'm not surprised.

PORTERHOUSE. She's lovely.

MARY. And she's perfectly happy about "Gruesome?"

PORTERHOUSE. After twenty years she ought to be.

MARY. *(Rises and moves in a pace.)* This is a real eye-opener! Does your "Gruesome" dress up like his "Lofty?"

PORTERHOUSE. Only when we go dancing together.

MARY. Dancing?!

(JOHN chokes on his tea. JOHN and STANLEY quickly rise. During the following lines. JOHN gives Stanley

his cup and Porterhouse's cup and STANLEY puts
them and his on the tray behind the settee. JOHN goes
to Porterhouse and pulls him up.)

JOHN. (*Hastily.*) That was a very nice cup of tea.

STANLEY. Yes it was, very nice.

JOHN. Thanks for the chat, too. And all the advice.

PORTERHOUSE. (*Cheerfully takes John DL.*) Oh.
Pleasure. I know how important a happy marriage is and
how difficult it can be adjusting in the early days.

JOHN. (*To Stanley.*) You see.

STANLEY. (*Moves DC. To Mary.*) You see.

MARY. (*Moves DRC.*) Well, I don't think I'm
prepared to adjust as much as Pussy's wife did.

PORTERHOUSE. Give and take. Now I'd like nothing
more than to see Mr. Smith (*He points to John.*) kiss and
make up with his "Lofty" – and for you (*HE goes in front
of Stanley to Mary.*) to have that morning in bed with
him. (*HE pulls Mary to him and joins her hands with
Stanley's.*)

MARY. (*Stony-faced.*) I see.

(*Looks across at Stanley. STANLEY tries to smile.*)

MARY. (*To Porterhouse.*) And you think that would
give me a happy marriage, do you?

PORTERHOUSE. Definitely, Mrs. Smith.

MARY. (*Calmly.*) Well, I think you're a perverted old
poof.

(*For a moment JOHN and STANLEY are too startled to
speak. PORTERHOUSE looks totally blank.
STANLEY gets John and pulls him over to
Porterhouse.*)

JOHN. (*To Porterhouse*.) Mrs. Smith is a bit upset, Sergeant. Remember—her grandparents.

(*There is a pause*.)

STANLEY. That was the *other* Sergeant.

JOHN. (*His face comes round to look at Stanley. Thinking very hard*.) Was it?

MARY. My grandparents?

JOHN. (*Hurries over to her at DRC*.) It's O.K.!

MARY. Has something happened to Granny and Grandad?

JOHN. No!

MARY. Then why did you mention them?

JOHN. Because I thought he (*Points to Porterhouse*.) would remember them, but of course, he wouldn't remember because he (*Points to Stanley*.) told the other one.

PORTERHOUSE. (*To Stanley*.) Why did Mrs. Smith call me a perverted old poof?

STANLEY. (*Flatly*.) Because she's upset about her grandparents.

PORTERHOUSE. (*Breaks R a pace, bemused*.) I see.

MARY. (*Hurries over to Stanley at DLC*.) John said they were O.K.

STANLEY. They are. They're staying with your brother, Sidney.

MARY. (*Confused*.) My brother Sidney?

STANLEY. Lives in Basingstoke!

MARY. (*More confused*.) Basingstoke?

STANLEY. Yes!

MARY. Stanley's potty!

PORTERHOUSE. (*Looks very surprised*.) Is he still using one of those?

(JOHN and STANLEY break upstage in despair as MARY briefly tries to grapple with Porterhouse's remark. It is too much for Mary and SHE breaks under the strain.)

MARY. *(Screaming.)* Ahhh!!!

(JOHN, STANLEY and PORTERHOUSE jump out of their skins.)

MARY. *(Screaming.)* Ahhhh! *(SHE stands there and starts to stamp her feet.)*

PORTERHOUSE. Oh my God! *(To Stanley.)* You'd better deal with her, sir.

(PORTERHOUSE pulls Stanley close to beside Mary, SHE looks up at Stanley.)

MARY. *(Screaming.)* Ahhh!
JOHN. *(Goes to Mary.)* Pull yourself together, "Mrs. Smith."
MARY. Ahhh!

(MARY screams and stamps her feet. JOHN and STANLEY attempt to calm her down. PORTERHOUSE backs away DL.)

PORTERHOUSE. It seemed to be Stanley's potty that set her off.

(Mary's screams become deep sobs. BOBBY enters from the bedroom.)

BOBBY. It's pouring through your bathroom ceiling! *(HE notices Mary.)* What's up with her?

JOHN. She's having hysterics.

BOBBY. She's worse than Cyril.

JOHN. Just look after your paint.

BOBBY. (*Moves to kitchen DL where Porterhouse is standing.*) I'll get a bucket from your kitchen. (*To Porterhouse.*) Excuse me, love. (*Pats Porterhouse's cheek and exits into kitchen.*)

PORTERHOUSE. Who the hell is that?

STANLEY. From upstairs.

MARY. (*Calls foolishly.*) Upstairs!

PORTERHOUSE. Shall I ring for a doctor?

JOHN. No! I think our friend here (*He indicates Stanley.*) should take her *home*.

(*JOHN crosses to Porterhouse and MARY collapses onto the C of settee. STANLEY sits beside her R end of settee, patting her hand.*)

PORTERHOUSE. She's in no fit state to go anywhere.

JOHN. Hang on, I've go those pills the hospital gave me. (*Takes bottle from pocket.*)

PORTERHOUSE. Is that advisable, sir?

JOHN. They're only for headaches. Can't do any harm. Get some water, will you?

(*JOHN sits L end of settee as PORTERHOUSE moves DL to kitchen. BOBBY enters from kitchen with a large plastic bowl.*)

BOBBY. (*Steps aside, to Porterhouse.*) One more dance and I really must go.

(*PORTERHOUSE gives him a look and exits into kitchen.*)

BARBARA. (*To John.*) Who is that?
JOHN. The police.
BOBBY. Oh, gawd help us all and Oscar Wilde!

(*JOHN and STANLEY are trying to revive the limp but
    moaning Mary.*
*PORTERHOUSE returns with a glass of water. HE comes
    to L. end of settee.*)

PORTERHOUSE. Water.

(*STANLEY leans over and takes glass. JOHN shakes a
    couple of pills from the bottle.*)

JOHN. Two should be O.K. (*To Mary.*) Drink that and
swallow these.
MARY. (*Still hysterical.*) Drink this—(*SHE takes the
glass of water.*)—and swallow these. (*SHE takes the bottle
from John instead of the proffered pills and "drinks" several
tablets from the bottle.*)
JOHN/STANLEY/PORTERHOUSE. (*Together.*) No!

(*But Mary has already swallowed from the bottle. SHE is
    lolling about and still moaning.*)

JOHN. Oh my God!
STANLEY. How many did she take?
JOHN. (*Surveying the bottle.*) About a dozen.
STANLEY. Bloody hell!
PORTERHOUSE. Make her sick.
JOHN. What?
PORTERHOUSE. Make her sick. Where's the
bathroom?
JOHN. Through there. (*To Stanley.*) Right, lift.

(*JOHN and STANLEY go to lift Mary but her legs collapse.*)

PORTERHOUSE. Come on!

(*PORTERHOUSE goes behind Mary and the three of them try to get hold of her but SHE has not totally lost control of her limbs.*
THEY all fall back onto the settee with Mary in their laps. BOBBY enters DR from bedroom. He has his sleeves rolled up ad he has red paint splash marks on this shirt and trousers. HE surveys the scene.)

BOBBY. Oh, it's an orgy!

PORTERHOUSE. It's nothing of the kind. She's swallowed some pills.

BOBBY. Make her sick!

PORTERHOUSE. Thank you! Salt water, Mr. Smith!

JOHN. Salt water, right! (*Hurries into the kitchen.*)

PORTERHOUSE. (*To Stanley.*) And some bicarbonate of soda and vinegar.

BOBBY. God, she'll explode!

PORTERHOUSE. (*Shouts to Stanley.*) Do as you're told, Mr. Smith.

STANLEY. All right!

BOBBY. (*To Stanley, brightly.*) Excuse me! Is your name Smith, as well?

STANLEY. Don't *you* bloody start!

(*STANLEY exits into kitchen DL. BOBBY exits into bedroom, leaving door open. As PORTERHOUSE gets Mary into a standing position, BARBARA enters behind him from hall URC. SHE still carries her suitcase which SHE puts down as SHE watches, bemused, while Porterhouse struggles with Mary.*

Finally PORTERHOUSE gets behind Mary and puts his feet against her. HE then "marches" her off into the bedroom with his arms around her waist. THEY exit with Mary bouncing up and down like a puppet but singing quite happily.

JOHN hurries in from kitchen with a glass of salt water and runs across into bedroom without noticing Barbara. Before Barbara can move, STANLEY hurries out of kitchen with bicarbonate of soda, vinegar and a bottle of tomato ketchup. HE rushes into the bedroom carrying the plastic bowl full of red distemper. HE goes through into the kitchen and exits.

BARBARA moves down, bewildered, as JOHN hurries in from the bedroom.

JOHN hurries towards kitchen and then stops. HE bangs the kitchen door shut and turns, horrified.)

JOHN. (*To Barbara.*) Lofty!

BARBARA. Lofty?

JOHN. (*Puts on a nonchalant air.*) Barbara! You're supposed to be staying in a hotel. (*Puts his arms around her lovingly.*)

BARBARA. Well, it all seemed pretty silly, really, darling.

JOHN. No. Very good idea. I'll join you there later. (*HE pushes her R and then rushes to kitchen door DL.*)

BARBARA. (*Moves to him.*) Hang on. What's going on here?

JOHN. (*Suddenly feigns total relaxation and leans against kitchen door.*) Nothing. Nothing doing at all.

BARBARA. There seems to be something doing in the bedroom.

JOHN. Bedroom?

BARBARA. That police sergeant just carried the nun through there.

JOHN. (*Crosses in front of her, thinking madly.*)

JOHN. Ah! Yes! I'd forgotten. She had a bit of a come-over.

BARBARA. (*Goes to him at C.*) How awful. What brought that on?

JOHN. We wouldn't donate. She became hysterical and then felt sick.

BARBARA. Good God.

JOHN. Yes. A sort of religious relapse.

BARBARA. (*Moves to bedroom.*) And what was that farmer doing?

JOHN. (*Moves to her and stops her.*) Ah! Well! Lucky he was still there. He's a bit of a vet.

BARBARA. (*Moves back to kitchen door DL.*) And what about Mr. Franklyn from upstairs? He looked like he's been giving a blood transfusion.

JOHN. (*Hurries to her.*) He's sorting out the paint that's coming through the ceiling. You go back to the hotel—

(*JOHN pulls her across him as BOBBY comes in from the kitchen with the plastic bowl now empty and carrying a "squeegy."*)

BOBBY. A woman's work is never done. (*To Barbara.*) Where have you been? All hell's been let loose here.

BARBARA. So I've been told.

BOBBY. (*Moves to bedroom door DR.*) I'm absolutely abject about the paint, darling.

BARBARA. Don't worry.

BOBBY. You'll worry when you see your bathroom. It looks like Sweeny Todd's cellar in there.

(*BOBBY exits into bedroom as STANLEY enters from bedroom.*)

STANLEY. John, you'd better come and deal with her—Lofty! (*Has just passed Barbara but then suddenly stops.*)

BARBARA. Lofty! (*Reacts.*)

STANLEY. You're supposed to be in a hotel.

JOHN. She thought it was silly.

BARBARA. (*To Stanley.*) How's your nun?

STANLEY. My what?

JOHN. How's *Sister Mary?*

STANLEY. (*Realizing.*) Oh! (*Sings reverently.*) "The hills are alive with the sound of Mary." (*Crosses to John DL with his hands held together in prayer.*)

JOHN. Is she feeling better?

STANLEY. I'm afraid she is, yes.

BARBARA. Did she explain why she wasn't wearing the usual sort of get up?

JOHN. (*Crosses to her at RC.*) Usual? Oh, yes! (*To Stanley.*) She's unorthodox, isn't she?

STANLEY. Very.

PORTERHOUSE. (*Enters from bedroom.*) She's swearing like a trooper!

(*BARBARA reacts.*)

PORTERHOUSE. (*Seeing Barbara.*) Oh, hello, Mrs. Smith.

BARBARA. How is she?

PORTERHOUSE. Well, she's still feeling pretty rotten. Do you think she could rest up on your bed for a bit?

BARBARA. Certainly.

(*BARBARA exits into bedroom. JOHN hurries over to Porterhouse.*)

JOHN. Ooo!

(*PORTERHOUSE looks surprised.*)

JOHN. That wasn't a very good idea.

PORTERHOUSE. Why not?

JOHN. Well, we don't want his Mrs. Smith getting violent with my Mrs. Smith or my Mrs. Smith getting violent with his Mrs. Smith.

PORTERHOUSE. Why should *either* of them get violent?

(*There is a loud SCREAM from Mary offstage. The MEN freeze. MARY rushes in from the bedroom. She is minus her dress and wears bra and pants. SHE is still slightly "dozey" but very angry. SHE turns to the open bedroom door.*)

MARY. (*Calls.*) Don't you try any of your fun and games with *me*, Lofty.

BARBARA. (*Appears in the doorway. SHE looks bewildered.*) What on earth did I do?

MARY. You took my dress off!

BARBARA. Only so that I could get you into bed.

MARY. (*To John.*) Blimey, talk about ambidextrous.

JOHN. It's all a bit of a misunderstanding.

STANLEY. Would you like to put that in writing?

PORTERHOUSE. I'll sort out her dress. (*Exits into bedroom*)

MARY. (*Calls after him.*) It won't fit you, Pussy!

JOHN. (*Goes to Mary.*) Just relax.

BARBARA. (*To Mary.*) Yes, you relax. Sister.

MARY. (*To Barbara.*) Don't you call me "Sister." (*Pulls away to C.*)

JOHN. (*To Barbara.*) She's probably still a novice, you see.

MARY. In this company, I bloody well am!

BARBARA. I've never heard such language.

PORTERHOUSE. (*Re-enters with Mary's dress and closes bedroom door.*) There we are.

MARY. (*Goes DR and snatches the dress from Porterhouse.*) God, if the Vice Squad knew about you lot! (*Moves UR and proceeds to get into her dress.*)

PORTERHOUSE. (*Referring to Mary.*) I'm sure her behaviour all stems from her relationship with Stanley.

BARBARA. Stanley?!

MARY. (*Moves down to Stanley.*) It damn well does!

BARBARA. (*To Mary.*) Do you know Stanley?

MARY. Yes, I do but don't worry, you can keep him.

PORTERHOUSE. No, no, no. You must think seriously before you have the little lad adopted.

(*THEY all look at Stanley who tries to look coy.*)

JOHN. (*Finally, to Mary.*) I'll drive you to the convent.

MARY. What the hell do I want to go to a convent for?

STANLEY. I think it could be the solution for all of us. (*HE lays on the settee and sucks his thumb like a child.*)

PORTERHOUSE. I'm convinced that Stanley's at the bottom of everything.

MARY. (*Moves to Porterhouse DR.*) Too bloody true, Pussy!

BARBARA. (*Moves in to John.*) Is this all because you wouldn't give her a donation?

MARY. What he gives me is a damn sight more natural than what he gives—

JOHN. (*Quickly cutting in.*) Sister Mary, please!

PORTERHOUSE. Sister? (*To Mary, referring to John.*) Is Mr. Smith your brother?!

MARY. (*Hesitates, then gives a similar scream to before, and runs DL.*) Ahhh!

(*JOHN, STANLEY, BARBARA and PORTERHOUSE all react. PORTERHOUSE pulls Stanley DL, Mary's side, and thrusts him at her.*)

PORTERHOUSE. Show her some affection or something!

STANLEY. (*After some hesitation. Pats her head.*) Hello!

(*MARY screams and stamps her feet.*)

BARBARA. (*To John.*) Is this how she was behaving before?

JOHN. Yes. (*HE indicates that Mary is mad.*)

BARBARA. (*Moves to C.*) It's obviously disturbing her, this unorthodox business of hers.

PORTERHOUSE. Well! I reckon that, too. (*To Stanley.*) It's not natural these two agreeing to have no sex.

(*MARY screams and rushes into bedroom DR.*)

JOHN. (*Finally, politely.*) Excuse me. (*Goes into bedroom after Mary.*)

BARBARA. Sergeant, really! That was very indelicate.

PORTERHOUSE. Well! (*To Stanley.*) That's what her trouble is. Not getting her rations.

BARBARA. She doesn't want any "rations." She's married to "Him."

(*SHE looks upwards to heaven. Porterhouse is astonished. PORTERHOUSE looks up and then at Stanley. STANLEY looks upwards, thinking.*)

STANLEY. (*After a pause.*) They're divorced now.

(*PORTERHOUSE and BARBARA think about this. The front DOORBELL goes.*)

BARBARA. Excuse me. (*Hurries into the hall URC.*)
PORTERHOUSE. (*To Stanley.*) Your wife used to be married to that fellow who lives up there?
STANLEY. Yes.
PORTERHOUSE. You mean—(*HE flicks his wrist.*) him?
STANLEY. Surprising, isn't it?
PORTERHOUSE. It's *amazing*. And is Stanley his son or yours?
STANLEY. His.
PORTERHOUSE. So you're Stanley's *step*-father?
STANLEY. Yes. On my mother's side.
PORTERHOUSE. Well, that explains Stanley's psychological problems.

(*BARBARA returns with Troughton.*)

BARBARA. (*To Troughton.*) I'll tell Mr. Smith you'd like to see him.
TROUGHTON. Thanks. Sorry to interrupt your cleaning.

(*BARBARA frowns and then goes into bedroom. TROUGHTON moves to DRC.*)

TROUGHTON. (*To Stanley, coldly.*) Still here, I see.

STANLEY. It's become a way of life, really.

(*STANLEY breaks ULC. TROUGHTON and PORTERHOUSE advance on each other and meet DC.*)

TROUGHTON. (*To Porterhouse.*) May I ask you who you are, sir?
PORTERHOUSE. May I ask who *you* are?
STANLEY. (*Steps in a pace. To Porterhouse.*) He *did* ask you first.

(*PORTERHOUSE turns on Stanley. STANLEY sits in chair DL.*)

TROUGHTON/PORTERHOUSE. Who are you?/Who are you?

(*There is a pause.*)

TROUGHTON/PORTERHOUSE. I'm a police officer./I'm a police officer.

(*There is a pause.*)

TROUGHTON. Let's start again. I'm Detective Sergeant Troughton, Wimbledon C.I.D.
PORTERHOUSE. Oh. I'm Detective Sergeant Porterhouse, Streatham C.I.D.
TROUGHTON. Oh. (*Doubtfully.*) Are you here in an official capacity?
PORTERHOUSE. Sort of semi. You?
TROUGHTON. Sort of semi. You're from Streatham, you say?
PORTERHOUSE. That's right.
TROUGHTON. May I see your identification, please?

PORTERHOUSE. (*Cooly.*) Certainly. (*Feels inside his jacket.*) Oh, I don't seem to have it on me. Like I said, this is only semi-official.

TROUGHTON. (*Dubiously.*) I see.

PORTERHOUSE. May I see your identification, please?

TROUGHTON. Certainly! (*Produces his Pass triumphantly and shows it to Porterhouse.*)

(*There is a scream from the bedroom.*)

MARY. (*Off.*) Ahh!

(*THEY all stop and turn. MARY rushes in from the bedroom. She is in bra and pants once more and carrying her dress.*)

MARY. (*Shouting into bedroom.*) You don't give up, do you, Lofty?! (*SHE sees Troughton and moves to him. During the ensuing dialogue SHE proceeds to put her dress back on. To Troughton.*) Thank God you're here.

TROUGHTON. Well, I only came to tell Mr. Smith we wouldn't be taking the matter any further.

MARY. Take it as far as you like. This is a right "porno" place, this is.

TROUGHTON. "Porno" place?

PORTERHOUSE. (*Steps in.*) I know a little about Mrs. Smith's situation, Sergeant—

(*TROUGHTON looks at Porterhouse.*)

PORTERHOUSE. (*To Troughton.*) The poor girl's got this obsession with sex.

MARY. Hark who's talking!

PORTERHOUSE. She's cut herself off, you see.

MARY. Pity *you* haven't!

PORTERHOUSE. It's all very understandable.

TROUGHTON. (*To Porterhouse.*) Is it? Well, I'd like you to remain silent until I've checked you out. (*Sits Porterhouse in L corner of settee.*)

PORTERHOUSE. Checked me out?!

MARY. Yes! Ask him about his dance routine with Gruesome.

JOHN. (*Hurries in from bedroom in a panic.*) For God's sake there's all hell—(*Sees Troughton.*) Oh, Sergeant!

TROUGHTON. (*Moves over to John DR. Coldly.*) Good morning again, Mr. Smith.

BARBARA. (*Enters from bedroom crosses John and stands by Troughton. In disbelief.*) That sister hit me.

MARY. (*Moves in to the other side of Troughton.*) And you'll get another one if you touch me again, Lofty.

TROUGHTON. (*To Mary.*) Is this lady your sister?

MARY. Lady?! (*To Barbara.*) Come on, show us your boobs, I dare you!

TROUGHTON. Hang on, hang on!

BARBARA. Let's just right the Mother Superior and get her out of here.

TROUGHTON. Mother who?!

MARY. (*Moves up and sits on R arm of settee.*) I'm staying where I am, Lofty.

PORTERHOUSE. It's little Stanley and her ex-husband that's caused all this.

TROUGHTON. (*Moves UR above settee to them DLC.*) I've asked you to be quiet, sir.

BARBARA. (*Moves to C below settee. To Troughton.*) Are you a police officer?

TROUGHTON. Yes, I am!

STANLEY. (*Rising.*) May *I* say something?

TROUGHTON. No, you may not, Mr. Gardner.

STANLEY. (*Indicating John.*) Then may Mr. Smith
say something?

JOHN. (*Steps in a pace.*) No, he may not, Mr. Gardner.

(*TROUGHTON glares at John and JOHN steps back a
pace.*)

PORTERHOUSE. (*Rising, to John, referring to
Stanley.*) Why are you calling Mr. Smith, Mr. Gardner?

TROUGHTON. (*To Porterhouse.*) Shut up!

BARBARA. (*To Porterhouse.*) You just called him.
(*SHE points to Stanley.*) "Mr. Smith."

PORTERHOUSE. Yes, he's a taxi driver from
Wimbledon.

TROUGHTON. Taxi driver?

BARBARA. He's a farmer from Gatwick.

TROUGHTON. Farmer?

MARY. He's a pansy from way back.

TROUGHTON. That much I know!

STANLEY. May *I* say something?!

TROUGHTON/JOHN. No!/No!

(*TROUGHTON glares at John. JOHN gives him a weak
wave.*)

PORTERHOUSE. Now, if Stanley's step-father is a
pansy as well, that *would* affect the little lad.

(*THEY all turn slowly to look at PORTERHOUSE who
sits again, L end of settee.*)

TROUGHTON. Look, I intend to make some sense out
of this. (*To John.*) Mr. Smith!

JOHN. That's me.

PORTERHOUSE. (*Rises. Points to Stanley.*) And *him*.

TROUGHTON. Belt up!

PORTERHOUSE. There are two of them.

TROUGHTON. I can *see* that.

PORTERHOUSE. Two "Smiths" I mean.

TROUGHTON. (*Angrily.*) That's their cover-up for the homosexual activities going on here.

BARBARA. What homosexual activities?

MARY. (*Rises.*) You take the cake, Lofty!

TROUGHTON. The activities between him and him. (*He points to John and Stanley.*)

BARBARA. What?!

TROUGHTON. They've admitted it.

BARBARA. (*In disbelief.*) But they've only just met.

PORTERHOUSE. Yes, I introduced them.

(*TROUGHTON slowly looks at him PORTERHOUSE realizes the implications and sits again.*)

TROUGHTON. (*To Porterhouse.*) I'm beginning to see where you fit in, Pussy.

BARBARA. (*Advances on John DR.*) Why don't *you* say something?!

STANLEY. (*Moves in to DLC.*) Yes, *say* something!

JOHN. I'm trying to *think* of something!

BARBARA. (*Moves in to John.*) I bet the pair of you have been meeting on that farm for ages.

(*MARY steps down to Barbara's R.*)

MARY. (*To Barbara.*) Go on, eat your heart out!

STANLEY. I want to confess!

JOHN. You've confessed already, shut up!

STANLEY. A *proper* confession.

JOHN. (*Points to Troughton.*) He'll decide what's proper.

STANLEY. John, we've *had* it.

JOHN. Everybody *knows* that!

BARBARA. (*Suddenly lets out a long wail.*) Ahhh!

(*EVERYBODY reacts. STANLEY breaks up to L end of settee. PORTERHOUSE runs to DL chair and sits.*)

TROUGHTON. (*To Barbara.*) What the devil's the matter with you?

BARBARA. (*Grabs John.*) My lovely John!

TROUGHTON. (*Heaves John across him to DLC. Bemused.*) *Your* lovely John?! (*To John.*) Don't tell me you've been giving the cleaning lady one as well?!

MARY. Cleaning lady? You mean the handyman!

(*BARBARA wails and runs towards bedroom at DR.*)

MARY. Yes! That'll teach you for stealing John from me. (*BARBARA half stops crying.*)

BARBARA. (*Still crying.*) How could I steal him from a nun?

(*EVERYBODY looks at John. JOHN kneels and "prays" for help. TROUGHTON walks DL looking at John.*)

MARY. A nun?! (*To John.*) Is that what you've been saying about me? Just because I like my sex normal? (*Runs towards door URC.*)

JOHN. (*Rises.*) Mary!

(*JOHN starts to move below settee towards Mary.*)

BARBARA. Sex?!

(*JOHN stops at R end of settee.*)

BARBARA. (*To John.*) Where the hell can you go after farmers and nuns?! (*Rushes into bedroom wailing.*)
JOHN. Barbara!

(*JOHN runs after her but BOBBY enters from bedroom and JOHN "about turns" to finish up R end of settee. Bobby is now covered in red paint.*)

BOBBY. Well, that's it. The whole bloody ceiling's in the bath now!
TROUGHTON. (*Approaches Bobby at DR.*) And who the bloody hell are you?
BOBBY. Who wants to know, sunshine?
TROUGHTON. (*Impassively.*) Detective Sergeant Troughton, sunshine.
BOBBY. (*Gaily.*) Whoopsy-poo!
TROUGHTON. So where do you fit in?
BOBBY. I practically live here now!
TROUGHTON. (*Looks at John and Stanley.*) I see!

(*JOHN and STANLEY are demolished. THEY sit on settee.*)

BOBBY. I've got the flat above normally. (*Laughing.*) "Normally!"
TROUGHTON. (*To Bobby.*) So you live upstairs?
BOBBY. With Cyril.
TROUGHTON. Cyril, I see! (*Looks at John and Stanley, who bury their heads.*)
PORTERHOUSE. (*To Stanley.*) I say. Is Cyril Stanley's brother?

(EVERYONE slowly looks at Porterhouse.)

PORTERHOUSE. Well, I'm confused about a lot of things, but I'm sure Stanley should have been off that potty years ago.

TROUGHTON. *(Yelling.)* Shut up, Pussy! *(To Bobby.)* And what do you and Cyril do exactly?

BOBBY. If ever we get around to it, we make frocks.

TROUGHTON. You make—? *(To John.)* A right bloody nest, this place is. *(To Bobby.)* You—back in the bathroom.

BOBBY. I don't think there's anything more I can—

TROUGHTON. *(Shouting.)* Do as you're told!

BOBBY. Bossy boots! *(Hurriedly returns into the bedroom. There is a silence.)*

JOHN. *(Rises.)* I think the time has come.

STANLEY. *(Rising.)* I think the time came hours ago.

JOHN. I should have listened to you earlier, Stanley. It would have saved a lot of heartache.

STANLEY. *(Doubtfully.)* Yes. Well, that's what I said.

JOHN. You did. *(To Troughton.)* He did. O.K., here we go—

STANLEY. The truth.

JOHN. Of course.

STANLEY. The whole truth.

JOHN. And nothing but.

(JOHN indicates for Stanley and Troughton to sit. THEY do so. STANLEY sits L end of settee. TROUGHTON sits in chair DR.)

JOHN. Firstly, I would like to dispel the rumour that the young lady who just rushed out in a flood of tears is a nun. This is a concoction entirely of my own making. Nor is she married to Mr. Gardner—who does not have a disturbed schoolboy son called Stanley. And for those who have been led to believe otherwise, Mr. Gardner practices neither as a farmer nor as a homosexual. Nor any any combination of the two.

Secondly, I wish it to go on record that the charming but hysterical lady through there is neither my daily help nor is she a transvestite—

Finally, I would like to say that all the aforementioned "Little White Lies" were contrived by me for the simple purpose of covering up my guilty secret—I am married to that lady in there and live here. At the same time I am married to the other lady and live somewhere else. Correct, Stanley? (*During the above speech JOHN has circled the stage telling his story. HE starts above chair DR and finishes below settee at C.*)

STANLEY. (*Rising, sadly.*) Correct, John. (*Puts his arm around John in comfort. There is a pause as THEY look at Troughton.*)

TROUGHTON. (*Finally.*) You lying bastard!

(*JOHN takes this in and then slowly looks around blankly at STANLEY who is standing there dumbfounded. John's face breaks into a smile. STANLEY starts to cry. JOHN kisses him.*
MUSIC - Love and Marriage. *
As the music starts the curtain begins to descend.)

CURTAIN

---

*See cautionary note in front matter.

FURNITURE AND PROPERTY LIST
ACT I

Onstage:

Table
Settee On it: cushions
Table L. On it: Mary's phone. In drawer:
         notepad, 3 pens
Table R. On it: Barbara's phone
2 armchairs
2 wastebins
Window curtains L. closed
Window R (practical) with curtain (or ..
         blinds closed)
Table under L window
Table under R window. On it: Barbara's
         handbag
Key in kitchen door
Key in bedroom door
    IN KITCHEN
Kitchen units (dressing only)
    IN BEDROOM
Dressing table and stool (dressing only)

Offstage:

Mug of tea (Mary)
Tray containing cup and saucer, plate, ..
         knife (Barbara)
Bottle of washing-up liquid
Mug of coffee (Mary)
Tumbler of water (Mary)
Tea towel (Mary)
Flask and lunch box (Mary)
Camera, flash-unit (practical), camera bag
         (Reporter)
Barbara's dress and shoes (John)
Barbara's shoes (Barbara)
Copy of *The Standard* (Stanley)

Tray containing pint of milk and 2 slices
of chocolate cake on plates
(Barbara)
Copy of *The Standard* (Barbara)
Tray containing 2 clean plates (Bobby)

Personal: Mary: wristwatch, wedding ring
Barbara: wristwatch, wedding ring
Troughton: notebook, pen, small bottle
of tablets, wristwatch
John: head bandage, diary, wristwatch
Porterhouse: notebook, handkerchief

ACT II

Strike: Paper from DL wastebin
Offstage: Tray containing 2 mugs of coffee
(Barbara)
Paint roller covered in red paint (Bobby)
Suitcase (Barbara)
Kettle (Porterhouse)
Tray containing tea set for 4
(Porterhouse)
Large plastic bowl, rubber gloves
(Bobby)
Glass of water (Porterhouse)
Suitcase (Barbara)
Glass of water, carton of sale (John)
Bicarbonate of soda, vinegar, bottle of ..
tomato ketchup (Stanley)
Plastic bowl full of red distemper
(Bobby)
Emptied bowl of distemper, squeegee ...
(Bobby)
Mary's dress (Porterhouse)
Mary's dress (Mary)

Personal:

John: head bandage, wristwatch, small
                bottle of tablets,
            handkerchief
Troughton: wristwatch, identity card
Barbara: wristwatch, wedding ring
Mary: wristwatch, wedding ring
Porterhouse: Barbara's apron
Stanley: handkerchief

RUN FOR YOUR WIFE

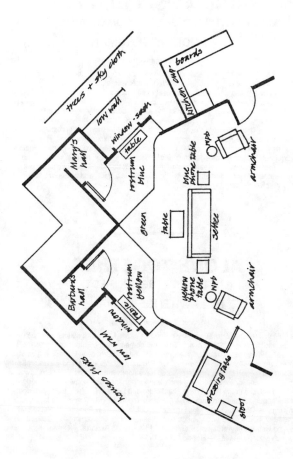

Other Publications for Your Interest

SOCIAL SECURITY
(LITTLE THEATRE—COMEDY)
By ANDREW BERGMAN

3 men, 3 women—Interior

This is a real, honest-to-goodness hit Broadway comedy, as in the Good Old Days of Broadway. Written by one of Hollywood's top comedy screenwriters ("Blazing Saddles" and "The Inlaws") and directed by the great Mike Nichols, this hilarious comedy starred Marlo Thomas and Ron Silver as a married couple who are art dealers. Their domestic tranquility is shattered upon the arrival of the wife's goody-goody nerd of a sister, her up-tight CPA husband and her Archetypal Jewish Mother. They are there to try to save their college student daughter from the horrors of living only for sex. The comic sparks really begin to fly when the mother hits it off with the elderly minimalist artist who is the art dealers' best client! "Just when you were beginning to think you were never going to laugh again on Broadway, along comes *Social Security* and you realize, with a rising feeling of joy, that it is once more safe to giggle in the streets. Indeed, you can laugh out loud, joyfully, with, as it were, social security, for the play is a hoot, and better yet, a sophisticated, even civilized hoot."—NY Post.   (#21255)

ALONE TOGETHER
(LITTLE THEATRE—COMEDY)
By LAWRENCE ROMAN

4 men, 2 women—Interior

Remember those wonderful Broadway comedies of the fifties and sixties, such as *Never Too Late* and *Take Her, She's Mine*? This new comedy by the author of *Under the Yum Yum Tree* is firmly in that tradition. Although not a hit with Broadway's jaded critics, *Alone Together* was a delight with audiences. On Broadway Janis Paige and Kevin McCarthy played a middle aged couple whose children have finally left the nest. They are now alone together—but not for long. All three sons come charging back home after experiencing some Hard Knocks in the Real World—and Mom and Dad have quite a time pushing them out of the house so they can once again be *alone together*. "Mr. Roman is a fast man with a funny line."—Chr. Sci. Mon. "A charmer."—Calgary Sunday Sun. "An amiable comedy . . . the audience roared with recognition, pleasure and amusement."—Gannett Westchester Newsp. "Delightfully wise and witty." Hollywood Reporter. "One of the funniest shows we've seen in ages."—Herald-News. TV.   (#238)